A GAME OF MURDER

MURDER

Francis Durbridge

WILLIAMS & WHITING

Cover design by Timo Schroeder

9781912582945

Williams & Whiting (Publishers)
15 Chestnut Grove, Hurstpierpoint,
West Sussex, BN6 9SS

Titles by Francis Durbridge published by Williams & Whiting

Murder At The Weekend – the rediscovered newspaper serials and short stories

Also published by Williams & Whiting:
Francis Durbridge : The Complete Guide
By Melvyn Barnes

Titles by Francis Durbridge to be published by Williams & Whiting

Breakaway – The Family Affair
Breakaway – The Local Affair
Johnny Washington Esquire
Murder On The Continent (Further re-discovered serials and stories)
One Man To Another – a novel
Operation Diplomat
Paul Temple and the Alex Affair
Paul Temple and the Canterbury Case (film script)
Paul Temple and the Conrad Case
Paul Temple and the Geneva Mystery
Paul Temple and the Jonathan Mystery
Paul Temple and the Lawrence Affair
Paul Temple and the Margo Mystery
Paul Temple and the Vandyke Affair
Paul Temple: Two Plays For Radio Vol 2 (Send For Paul Temple and News of Paul Temple)
The Man From Washington
The Passenger
Tim Frazer and the Salinger Affair
Tim Frazer and the Mellin Forrest Mystery

INTRODUCTION

Francis Durbridge (1912-98) was arguably the most popular writer of mystery thrillers for BBC radio from the 1930s to the 1960s. In 1938 he found the formula that was to establish his name, when his radio serial *Send for Paul Temple* proved so successful that subsequent Paul Temple serials over several decades were enthusiastically received by an impressive number of UK and European fans.

It was therefore not surprising that Durbridge turned to television while continuing to write for radio – and he did so in fine style by writing the first thriller serial on UK television, *The Broken Horseshoe* (1952). Much later, in a published interview (*Radio Times*, 21 October 1971) Durbridge said: "Twenty years ago in the United States, a producer told me that I was wasting my time by not going into television. So that's what I did – I tried to build up a reputation with serials, since I'd vowed never to write a Paul Temple episode for television."

A Game of Murder was Durbridge's thirteenth television serial, transmitted in six thirty-minute episodes from 26 February to 2 April 1966, although it could legitimately be counted as his fifteenth because *The World of Tim Frazer* (1960-61) had consisted of three interlinked serials of six episodes each. *A Game of Murder* was later repeated (25 October to 29 November 1968), when the *Radio Times* quoted two press comments about the original screening. "Mr Durbridge, with his own virtuosity, cooked up a situation of endless potentialities and baffling mystifications. Like all his work, it will leave us no peace until we know the answer," said *The Times*; and "The question is not whether the story's suspense will keep taut, but whether we can be suspended for so many weeks without snapping," said the *Daily Sketch*.

The producer/director, Alan Bromly, had been the guru for most of Durbridge's television serials from *Portrait of Alison* in 1955. Bromly and Durbridge delighted in teasing viewers in ways that became familiar – numerous red herrings, a cliff-hanger ending to each episode, and the certainty that most characters were out to deceive. The plots usually concerned a protagonist struggling in a vicious web spun by a killer who remained concealed until the final episode, enthralling viewers for nearly thirty years and branding Francis Durbridge as the pre-eminent practitioner of the thriller serial on UK television.

But Durbridge also exuded the quality of "Britishness", which distinguished his work from American television imports that often relied upon car chases, gunplay and "sock-in-the jaw" action rather than sophistication. In fact his Britishness was probably the element that had already given him since the late 1930s an enviable reputation in Europe, with translations of his radio serials broadcast in various countries using their own actors. And then came television, beginning with *The Other Man* (1959 in Germany as *Der Andere*) followed by numerous Continental productions that attracted a huge body of viewers. Indeed the addictiveness of Durbridge on radio and television in Europe resulted in German commentators defining his serials as *straßenfeger* (street sweepers), because so many people stayed at home to listen to them on the radio or watch them on television.

In the case of *A Game of Murder*, the Italian television version was *Giocando a golf una mattina* (28 September – 16 October 1969, six episodes), translated by Franca Cancogni and directed by Daniele D'Anza; the French television version was *La Mort d'un champion* (4 – 5 February 1972, two episodes), translated and directed by Abder Isker; the Polish television version was *Brutalna gra* (30 September – 14 October 1976, three episodes), translated by Kazimierz Piotrowski and directed by Anna Minkiewicz; and the German television version was *Die Kette* (18 – 20 December 1977, two episodes), translated by Marianne de Barde and Hubert von Bechtolsheim and directed by Rolf von Sydow.

Although a recording of *A Game of Murder* clearly existed, it took until 2014 for it to become available on DVDs (BBC/Danann), and this was later included in the DVD box set *Francis Durbridge Presents Volume 1* (BBC/Madman, 2016). Indeed the title of the set *Francis Durbridge Presents* is significant in itself, because it defines a crucial aspect of Durbridge's career – with his success in television drama becoming monumental, he reaped the reward that for all his serials from 1960 onwards (beginning with *The World of Tim Frazer*) the BBC gave him the unprecedented accolade of the "Francis Durbridge Presents" screen credit before the title sequence of each episode.

On UK television *A Game of Murder* – as usual for a Durbridge serial – boasted a superb cast. The leading man was Gerald Harper (born 1929, although some sources say 1931), who soon afterwards secured iconic television status in *Adam Adamant Lives!* (1966-67) and later starred as the long-running television *Hadleigh* (1969-76), and who had already appeared in Durbridge's immediately preceding television serial *A Man Called Harry Brent* (22 March to 26 April 1965). In fact Gerald Harper became closely associated with Durbridge, as on the West End stage he was the leading man in the Durbridge plays *Suddenly at Home* (1971-73) and *House Guest* (1981-82). Also appearing in *A Game of Murder* was Conrad Phillips (1925-2016), for whom the 1960s and 1970s was his busiest period in the theatre, television and films – and who is still remembered today for the 1958-59 television series *The Adventures of William Tell*.

As with many of Francis Durbridge's radio and television scripts, *A Game of Murder* was novelised (Hodder & Stoughton, February 1975). For no apparent reason most of the character names were changed from those in the original television serial, and in particular Detective Inspector Jack Kerry became Detective Inspector Harry Dawson. These name changes, interestingly, were subsequently adopted in the 1977 German television version *Die Kette* mentioned above. While in Germany the novel was published as *Die Kette*, in Italy it was *Giocando a golf una mattina*, in Norway it was *Spillet om mord*, in Poland it was *Mordercza gra* and in Croatia it was *Smrtonosna igra*.

Melvyn Barnes
Author of *Francis Durbridge: The Complete Guide* (Williams & Whiting, 2018)

This book reproduces Francis Durbridge's original script together with the list of characters and actors of the BBC programme on the dates mentioned, but the eventual broadcast might have edited Durbridge's script in respect of scenes, dialogue and character names.

A GAME OF MURDER

A serial in six episodes
By FRANCIS DURBRIDGE
Broadcast on BBC Television
26 February – 2 April 1966
CAST:

Douglas Croft . . . . Christopher Wray
Liz Mason . . . . Lesley Carole
Bob Kerry . . . . .Anthony Sagar
Det Insp Jack Kerry . . . . . . .Gerald Harper
Freda Lincoln . . . . .Dorothy Frere
P.C. Collier . . . . Donald Oliver
Rupert Delaney . . . . Murray Hayne
Det Insp Ed Royce . . . . .David Burke
Iris Bannister . . . . .Diana King
Charles Bannister . . . . .John Harvey
Cathy White . . . . June Barry
Chief Supt. Bromford . . . . Conrad Phillips
Postman . . . . Bernard G. High
Norman Penn. . . . . .Peter Copley
P.C. Hodges. . . . . .Alan Lynton
Brenda Thompson . . .Elizabeth Hopkinson
Doreen Osborne . . . . Dorothy White
Taxi driver . . . . Bernard Stone
Taxi driver . . . . Derek Martin
Cleg Reed . . . . Kenneth Hendel
Leonard Lincoln . . . . .John Carlin
Barman . . . . Richard Jacques
Det.-Insp. Everson . . . . Donald Hoath
Dr. Hasling . . . . .Kenneth Waller
Dr. Friedman . . . . Christopher Gilmore
Greta . . . . .Patricia Shakesby
Sergeant Fuller . . . . .Brian Cant
P.C. Small . . . . Reg Whitehead

EPISODE ONE

OPEN TO: Outside Bob Kerry Ltd – a prosperous sports shop situated at Swiss Cottage, near Lords Cricket Ground, London. The shop windows are well stocked with sports equipment of all kinds and there is a large blown-up action photograph of the great sportsman himself, Bob Kerry. The photograph was taken many years ago, in Kerry's hey-day, when he played cricket for England, was a Rugby International, and was twice runner-up in the British Open Golf Championship. Above the shop can be seen the curtained windows of the Kerry apartment. There is a private entrance to this flat on the extreme right of the shop.
DOUGLAS CROFT, a fair-haired, athletic looking man in his late twenties, arrives. He glances at the window display, then unlocks the front door of the shop and goes inside.

CUT TO: Bob Kerry Ltd. Day.
At the rear of this well-stocked prosperous looking shop, stands a small office – glass-partitioned off from the rest of the store. There is a spiral staircase which starts in the basement and continues through the office, to the Kerry apartment above.
DOUGLAS enters the shop, and after picking up the mail, crosses to the office. As DOUGLAS enters the office, he takes off his coat and hangs it on a coat-hanger just inside the door. There are two wall desks in the office, complete with telephone – one an intercom phone to the Kerry apartment, the other an outside line. We also see a medium sized safe, several filing cabinets, chairs, etc. DOUGLAS is glancing through the mail when the shop door opens and his assistant, LIZ MASON, arrives. LIZ is just nineteen, a pleasant girl, interested in sport and keen on her job. LIZ walks towards the office.

DOUGLAS: (*Looking up*) Good morning, Liz! Have a nice weekend?

LIZ: No, horrible!

LIZ takes off her coat.

LIZ: I lost every game on Saturday.

3

DOUGLAS: I told you not to wear those purple shorts!

LIZ: It wasn't the shorts. It was me! Isn't Mr Kerry down yet?

DOUGLAS: I think he's having the day off, he said something about it last week.

LIZ hangs up her coat.

LIZ: I'm told there was an article about him in The Sunday News. Did you see it?

DOUGLAS: Yes, they're running a series on famous sportsmen. I've read them all so far. It was a very good one on Mr Kerry – (*Amused*) except that they described his son as "the tough little glamour boy of Scotland Yard".

LIZ: What nonsense! Jack isn't tough – he's not as tough as his father.

There is a buzz on the intercom phone.

DOUGLAS: Here's the old boy now, by the sound of things.

DOUGLAS turns and picks up the phone.

DOUGLAS: (*On the phone*) Good morning, Mr Kerry.

CUT TO: The Living Room of the Flat. Morning.

The Kerry apartment, which is above the shop, consists of a living room, three bedrooms, a box room, kitchen, bathroom, etc. There is also an entrance hall, leading out of the living room, to the front door. When the front door is open, we can see the main staircase, which leads down to the private (street) entrance to the flat. One of the living room doors lead to the kitchen, JACK's bedroom, and the box room. (The spiral staircase from the office terminates in the box room).

The living room is well furnished but is obviously part of a male establishment, the emphasis being on comfort.

BOB KERRY is standing by an old-fashioned writing bureau talking to DOUGLAS on the intercom phone. There is also an outside phone on the desk. KERRY is a powerful looking man

4

*in his early sixties. His son, DETECTIVE-INSPECTOR JACK
KERRY, is sitting at the breakfast table reading a newspaper
and drinking a cup of coffee.*

KERRY: (*On the phone*) I shall probably be out all day,
           Douglas. If Harris Brothers phone just stall, I'll
           talk to them tomorrow.

CUT TO:

DOUGLAS: (*A letter in his hand*) Yes, all right, Mr Kerry.
           There's a reply from Allied Sports, it's not very
           satisfactory, I'm afraid.

CUT TO:

KERRY: What do they say? (*Changing his mind*) No,
           don't read it to me – bring it up. Oh, and bring
           me some golf balls, Douglas – you'd better make
           it half-a-dozen.

KERRY replaces the phone and returns to the breakfast table.

JACK: Who are you playing with today?

KERRY: (*Sitting down*) I'm not playing with anyone, I'm
           just going to have a knock round on my own.
           What are you doing, by the way – you start your
           leave today, don't you?

JACK: Yes, thank goodness! (*He stretches himself*)
           Gosh, to think I don't have to go near the Yard,
           or listen to old man Bromford, for two whole
           weeks!

KERRY: I get the impression you haven't been getting on
           too well with the Superintendent just lately,
           Jack.

JACK: Chief-Superintendent, if you don't mind. I've
           been getting on with him all right, he just hasn't
           been getting on with me. Still, Bromford's not a
           bad chap, I suppose – he's just an irritable old

cuss. By the way, Dad – I've changed my mind. I'm not going away after all, I'm just going to potter about for a couple of weeks, if that's okay with you.

KERRY: Sure – just please yourself, Jack.

JACK: I'm going over to Putney Hospital this morning to see a colleague of mine. He's a do-it-yourself enthusiast – or rather he was. The poor devil's broken his collar bone.

FREDA LINCOLN, the Kerry housekeeper, enters from the kitchen. Normally a determined looking woman, she now appears depressed and worried.

FREDA: Would you like some more toast, Mr Kerry?

JACK: No, thank you, Mrs Lincoln. We're nearly finished …

KERRY: There's no news of that dog of yours, I suppose?

FREDA: No, I'm afraid not. I rang the R.S.P.C.A. last night to see if they could help, but they couldn't of course. (*She shakes her head*) It's always the same – no one seems to bother, no one wants to know.

JACK: (*Irritated*) Well, we're bothering, Mrs Lincoln – we're doing everything we can. (*Indicating the newspaper*) The advertisement's in the local paper and they've even published the photograph I sent them.

JACK holds the paper up so that FREDA can see it. We see a picture of a handsome poodle on two legs, begging for a biscuit. The dog wears an ornate collar. The picture carries the caption: "Have You Seen Midge?"

FREDA: Yes, I know you're doing all you can, Mr Jack. I wasn't referring to you. But it's nearly a week now since Midge disappeared. (*Near to tears*) And he was wearing his collar, that's what I

6

	don't understand, Mr Kerry. He was wearing that lovely little collar you gave him.
KERRY:	(*Looking helplessly across to JACK*) Yes, well – never mind, Mrs Lincoln. Now come on, pull yourself together, it's not the end of the world.
JACK:	Cheer up, Mrs Lincoln!
KERRY:	(*Suddenly*) I think I'd like some more coffee. What about you, Jack?
JACK:	Yes. Good idea!

FREDA hesitates, then gives an understanding nod and returns to the kitchen.

KERRY:	That bloody poodle!
JACK:	She's making a meal of it, I'm afraid.
KERRY:	The trouble is, of course, she thinks <u>you</u> ought to be able to find him, just like that. (*He snaps his fingers*)
JACK:	(*Smiling*) Yes, I know. I must be the worst detective in England in her eyes.

CUT TO: The Box Room of the Flat. Morning.
This is a spare room, used for storing suitcases, out-dated office files, discarded sports equipment etc. The staircase, from the office below, terminates in a corner of this room.
DOUGLAS appears at the top of the spiral staircase and enters the room. He is carrying a box of golf balls, a manilla folder, and several letters. He crosses the room and knocks on the door leading into the living room.

CUT TO: The Living Room. Morning.
JACK and his father are still at the breakfast table. The box room door opens, and DOUGLAS appears.

DOUGLAS:	May I come in, sir?
KERRY:	Yes, of course. Come along in, Douglas.
DOUGLAS:	Good morning, Jack.

7

JACK: Hello, old boy!

DOUGLAS hands KERRY a letter and puts the golf balls on the table.

DOUGLAS: This is the Allied Sports letter, sir. And there's
               a reply from Houston's. He wants to drop in
               and see you.

KERRY: There's no point in him seeing me. The raquets
               were faulty, they've just got to take them back.

DOUGLAS opens the folder and looks at some notes.

DOUGLAS: … you've made a note for me to phone Swim-
               Dive; I don't know what about, sir.

KERRY: (*Studying the letter*) What? Oh, yes! Don't
               worry about that, Douglas – I've seen to it.

DOUGLAS looks at the cover of the folder.

DOUGLAS: And you've jotted down what … looks like …
               a car number, for some reason or other.

KERRY: (*Looking up*) A car number?

DOUGLAS: Yes … It's on the cover … 384 JKY.

KERRY: I don't know what on earth that is … Ask Liz
               about it, she probably wrote it down. (*He
               returns to the letter*) You know this letter from
               Allied really is a damned impertinence! It's
               just begging the issues.

KERRY looks at the letter, scowling at the contents. FREDA LINCOLN enters from the kitchen with a fresh supply of coffee.

DOUGLAS: Good morning, Mrs Lincoln.

FREDA: Oh, good morning.

DOUGLAS: Any news of Midge?

FREDA: No, no, I'm afraid not, Mr Croft. (*She is near
               to tears again*) Unfortunately.

KERRY glares at DOUGLAS, then glances across to JACK, his expression clearly saying – "Oh, my God, here we go again!"

8

CUT TO: Outside Putney Hospital. Morning.

An Austin 1100, driven by JACK, comes out of the main gate of the hospital and turns into the road. As it gathers speed, a police car suddenly appears from the direction of Putney and, racing past the Austin, pulls into the side of the road. Two uniformed men – LAWSON and COLLIER – jump out of the car and signal JACK's car into the kerb. Puzzled, JACK stops the Austin and gets out. The two police officers approach.

COLLIER: Mr Kerry?

JACK: Yes?

COLLIER: Inspector Royce has been trying to contact you, sir. There's been an accident – he wants you to go to the Highgate Golf Club.

JACK: An accident? What do you mean – what kind of an accident?

COLLIER: … I understand your father was hit by a golf ball, sir. Apparently, he was in a bunker and another player – a young chap called Delaney – didn't see him, so … (*He hesitates, then:*) I'm afraid your father was killed, Mr Kerry.

CUT TO: A Room at Highgate Golf Club, near London. Day.

RUPERT DELANEY is speaking to DETECTIVE INSPECTOR ED ROYCE and JACK. ED ROYCE is a rugged-looking man of about forty. He is a great friend of JACK's, but they frequently don't see eye to eye. RUPERT DELANEY is highly strung, very good-looking and obviously fond of clothes: he is in his early thirties. JACK is sitting in a chair, ED on the arm of a settee. RUPERT is standing facing them.

RUPERT: … I didn't see him … I didn't see him at all, otherwise of course, I wouldn't have taken the shot.

JACK: (*Angrily*) But didn't you see him on the fairway, before he got into the bunker?

9

RUPERT:	No, I'm afraid I didn't.
JACK:	Were you on your own?
RUPERT:	Yes, I was practising. I only had a number two iron with me.
ED:	(*To JACK*) This happened on the twelfth; it's only about a hundred and seventy yards long. The bunker's pretty high, it's right by the green.

JACK nods.

RUPERT:	Your father was already in the bunker when I reached the tee. He must have been, Mister Kerry.
JACK:	And how long was it before the doctor arrived?
RUPERT:	The Steward was out so I had to find the Pro … I'm afraid it was about an hour before the doctor got here.
JACK:	That's a hell of a long time!
RUPERT:	Yes, I know, sir, but it took me fifteen minutes to … to …

Lost for words, RUPERT glances across at ED.

ED:	Jack, the doctor agrees with Mister Delaney. Apparently, the ball hit your father on the back of the neck, he fell and struck his head on a stone. There are several of them in the bunker. We've examined the stone and the doctor says in his opinion …
JACK:	Look, I'm not interested in what the doctor says! If it took him an hour to get here what the hell does he know about it?
RUPERT:	Mister Kerry, I just don't know what to say to you. Believe me, if I could do anything … anything at all to …
JACK:	(*Abruptly*) Did you know my father?

RUPERT: No, I'd never seen him before. I knew of him, of course, and I'd always admired him. (*Tensely: overwrought*) My God, if anyone had told me this morning that this was going to happen I … I … Mister Kerry, I am most terribly … terribly distressed about this … I just don't know what I can say to you … (*Words fail him*)

JACK looks at RUPERT. He doesn't say anything.

ED: (*Quietly*) I think you said you wanted to make a phone call, Mister Delaney?

RUPERT: What …? Oh, yes …

ED: (*Nodding*) There's a box in the hall.

RUPERT: Thank you.

RUPERT looks at JACK, is about to say something else, then changes his mind and goes out into the hall.

ED: (*After a thought*) The Golf Professional phoned your office and they got in touch with me. I came out here straight away, Jack.

JACK nods, but his thoughts are obviously elsewhere.

JACK: Yes … Yes, thank you, Ed … I appreciate it …

CUT TO: BOB KERRY Ltd. Morning. A few days later.
DOUGLAS is in the office, sitting at his desk, examining a pile of invoices. There is a large suitcase on the floor by the side of his desk. LIZ is in the shop, saying goodbye to a customer. JACK enters the shop from the street. His manner is in keeping with his expression: tense; irritable. LIZ looks at him as he ignores her and crosses to the office. DOUGLAS looks up as JACK enters the office.

DOUGLAS: (*Surprised*) Is the Inquest over?

JACK: Yes.

DOUGLAS: That didn't take long.

JACK: Twelve and a half minutes, to be precise.

11

DOUGLAS:	What happened?
JACK:	(*With sarcasm*) The Coroner was a tidy little man with a tidy little mind. Death by misadventure.
DOUGLAS:	You sound as if you don't agree with the verdict.
JACK:	(*Looking at DOUGLAS*) I don't.
DOUGLAS:	You mean – you think Delaney was careless and the Coroner should have brought in ...
JACK:	Look, Doug, I'm sorry – if you don't mind – I don't want to talk about it! Not now.
DOUGLAS:	(*Quietly*) Yes, all right, Jack.

JACK looks at the suitcase.

JACK:	Whose is that?
DOUGLAS:	It's Mrs Lincoln's, she brought it down about five minutes ago. She's going away for a few days.
JACK:	(*Surprised*) Going away?
DOUGLAS:	Yes, her nephew's been taken ill. At least, I think she said her nephew.
JACK:	Our Leonard. He's with the Storm Insurance Company ...?
DOUGLAS:	That's right.

LIZ appears in the doorway.

LIZ:	Good morning, Mister Kerry.
JACK:	Hello, Liz.
LIZ:	(*Curious*) What happened at the Inquest?
DOUGLAS:	(*Quietly*) What we thought would happen.
LIZ:	Oh ... Oh, I see. (*To JACK*) Was he there? The young man – Delaney, I mean?
JACK:	Yes, he was there.
DOUGLAS:	Of course he was there, Liz. Don't be stupid.

FREDA LINCOLN suddenly appears, coming down the spiral staircase, carrying a zip bag. She is obviously surprised to find JACK in the office.

JACK:	Hello, Mrs Lincoln …
FREDA:	Oh … Oh, hello, Mister Kerry … I was hoping I'd see you. (*A shade embarrassed*) I'm afraid I've got to leave you for two or three days, sir.
JACK:	Yes, so Douglas has been telling me …
FREDA:	Leonard – my nephew – has been taken ill and unfortunately there's no one to look after him.
JACK:	Oh, I'm sorry to hear that. I hope it's not serious?
FREDA:	No, no, I don't think so, I think it's just the flu. Leonard has been very good to me, one way and another, and I should hate to think that I … I …
JACK:	Yes, of course …
FREDA:	I feel guilty leaving you, Mister Kerry – especially at a time like this.
JACK:	Not to worry, Mrs Lincoln. I'm quite capable of looking after myself for a few days.
LIZ:	Shall I get you a taxi, Mrs Lincoln?
FREDA:	Would you, Liz? This case is very heavy.
DOUGLAS:	I'll take it out for you.

DOUGLAS picks up the suitcase and goes out of the office with it, followed by LIZ.

FREDA:	(*To JACK*) I suppose there's been no news – about Midge, I mean? I hardly like to ask … with all the trouble you've had lately.
JACK:	No, I'm sorry, Mrs Lincoln. (*Shaking his head*) I saw the Sergeant this morning – they haven't heard anything.
FREDA:	And they won't either … Not now, I'm afraid … It's too late … He was killed … run over,

> Mister Kerry … I'm sure of it … (*Shaking her head*) Poor Midge …

FREDA goes out of the office. JACK stands watching her, then turns towards his father's desk. He is turning the pages of a diary, his thoughts elsewhere, when ED ROYCE speaks.

ED: May I come in?

JACK turns and finds ED in the doorway.

JACK: Hello, Ed.

ED: What happened to <u>you</u>? Why did you disappear so quickly?

JACK: I didn't want to hang around. I didn't feel like it.

ED: No one asked you to hang around. (*He moves toward JACK*) Jack, why didn't you acknowledge Delaney this morning when he spoke to you? That boy's in a state – one hell of a state – he has been ever since the accident.

JACK: (*Aggressively*) What "accident"?

ED: What do you mean – what "accident"? I'm talking about your father, about what happened on the golf course. (*Exasperated*) Jack, for God's sake! You heard Delaney's evidence, you heard what the doctor said – of course it was an accident!

JACK: I don't think it was. (*Quietly*) I never have thought so.

JACK crosses and sits down at his father's desk.

JACK: I'm sorry, Ed, I know you think I'm crazy but I'm entitled to my opinion.

ED: Of course you're entitled to your opinion – but if it wasn't an accident, what was it? Do you think Delaney murdered your father? Good God, the best golfer in the world couldn't be sure of hitting a man two hundred yards away,

14

especially if he was in a bunker. (*He moves nearer to JACK*) Jack, be reasonable – Delaney didn't know your father, he'd never even met him.

JACK: (*Quietly: deliberately*) I still don't think it was an accident.

ED hesitates, is about to say something, then gives a little shrug and turns away.

ED: You're coming to dinner on Friday night?

JACK: Yes, if it's okay.

ED: Of course it's okay. Rona's looking forward to it.

The telephone rings.

JACK: Eight o'clock.

ED: Any time after seven, the kids'll be in bed by then.

JACK: Thank you, Ed. Give my love to Rona.

ED goes out as JACK turns and picks up the phone.

CUT TO: The Drawing room of CHARLES BANNISTER's house at Hampstead. Morning.

This is a large, beautifully furnished room, reflecting not only wealth but also good taste.

IRIS BANNISTER is standing by a small table, on the phone. She is an attractive woman in her early fifties.

IRIS: Is that Juniper 1996?

CUT TO:

JACK: Yes …

CUT TO:

IRIS: My name is Bannister, Mrs Bannister. There's an advertisement in our local paper about a poodle   …

15

CUT TO:

JACK: Yes, that's right.

IRIS: Is the dog yours, Mr ...?

JACK: Kerry. No, it's my housekeeper's, but I'm responsible for the advertisement. (*Surprised*) Have you found the poodle, Mrs Bannister?

CUT TO:

IRIS: Yes. (*With a little laugh*) At least, I think so. It looks like the one in the paper – only a little dishevelled, I'm afraid. Actually, my husband found it last night, in the garden.

CUT TO:

JACK: Where are you, Mrs Bannister?

CUT TO

IRIS: We're in Hampstead. Stillwater, Lawrence Avenue ... Do you know Hampstead at all?

JACK: Yes, I do ...

IRIS: It's a large house, just on the corner, it stands back from the main road. The drive's on the right-hand side.

CUT TO:

JACK: Will you be in this morning?

CUT TO:

IRIS: Yes, we shall be here all day. You can drop in any time.

CUT TO:

JACK: Thank you, Mrs Bannister. It's very kind of you to have phoned.

As JACK replaces the phone he looks down at the desk. There is a copy of the local newspaper on the desk, showing the photograph of Midge.

CUT TO: The Drawing room of CHARLES BANNISTER's House at Hampstead. Morning.

JACK is sitting on the settee, the poodle in his arms, listening to CHARLES BANNISTER recount how Midge was discovered in the garden. CHARLES BANNISTER is in a wheelchair which he manipulates with dexterity, almost relish – he is a little younger than his wife; a spruce, meticulously dressed man. IRIS sits next to JACK, stroking the poodle – which is without a collar – she is only vaguely interested in what her husband is saying.

BANNISTER: … Naturally, I was surprised when I saw the animal. He was behind one of the rhododendron bushes, perfectly docile, almost asleep. I thought, well – blow me – how the devil did you get here!

JACK: He's been missing over a week now; we'd given up hope of ever seeing him again. (*To the dog*) Where have you been, Midge? What the devil happened to you?

IRIS: You say he was wearing a collar when he disappeared?

JACK: Yes, a very nice one. Mr father gave it to Mrs Lincoln for her birthday.

IRIS: (*Amused*) For <u>her</u> birthday, not the poodle's!

JACK: (*Laughing*) Yes …

BANNISTER moves to the settee.

BANNISTER: Some long-haired character picked him up in his car, I expect – then pinched the collar and booted him out. That's about it. (*He pats the poodle*) You've had a rough time, old boy, but

17

	I expect that mistress of yours will make up for it.
JACK:	That's the understatement of the year. (*Rising from the settee*) Mr Bannister, there was a reward mentioned in the paper, five pounds I think it was. Naturally, I'll be only too pleased to ...
IRIS:	(*Laughing*) Mr Kerry, please!
BANNISTER:	Don't be silly, old man! We're only too happy to have found the little chap. (*A sudden thought*) But wait a minute! (*Grinning*) I suppose you wouldn't like to give the fiver to charity?
IRIS:	Darling!
BANNISTER:	Now don't be squeamish, old girl! Why do you think they gave me the job? (*To JACK*) I'm President of the Hamsters, Mr Kerry – although I don't suppose you've heard of us.
JACK:	Er – no, I'm afraid I haven't.
BANNISTER:	We're a local society. What the Yanks would call "just a bunch of do-gooders". We help the old age pensioners, look after the poor kids of the district, put on the odd show when we feel like it – in aid of charity, of course. Last year we collected well over eight hundred pounds.

JACK turns and puts Midge back on the settee.

JACK:	Why, of course – I shall be delighted to give you a donation. (*He takes out his cheque book*)
BANNISTER:	Thank you, Mr Kerry.
IRIS:	Charles, you really are a monster!
BANNISTER:	Nonsense, Iris! Every bob counts these days, you know that. (*To JACK*) Make the cheque out to Basil Higgs, old man. He's our Secretary ... H.I. double G. S ...

IRIS takes hold of Midge.

IRIS: You can use the desk over there, Mr Kerry.

JACK: (*Crossing to the desk*) Thank you.

BANNISTER: I expect you'll hear from Basil. He's bound to drop you a line.

IRIS: (*Laughing*) You'll hear from him all right! Twice a year!

JACK smiles and, taking out his pen, sits down at the desk.

CUT TO: Finchley Road. Morning.

JACK comes out of a tobacconist's and crosses down to the car which is parked outside the shop.

CUT TO: JACK's car. Morning.

JACK gets into the car and looks down at the poodle which is resting in a basket on the back seat. JACK starts the car.

CUT TO: Finchley Road. Morning.

JACK's car slows down as it approaches a set of traffic lights on the Finchley Road.

CUT TO: JACK's car. Morning.

JACK is sitting at the wheel of his car waiting for the lights to change. As the green light appears a Fiat Estate car draws level with JACK's car. It is driven by RUPERT DELANEY. Sitting next to RUPERT is a pretty girl of about twenty-five – CATHY WHITE. RUPERT and the GIRL are obviously in the middle of an argument, and not a particularly friendly one at that. Neither of them is aware of the fact that JACK has now recognised RUPERT and is watching them. The Fiat surges forward and then drives away.

CUT TO: Through the windscreen of JACK's car.
JACK is staring at the registration number of the Fiat – 384 JKY – as the car races ahead, finally disappearing into the traffic.

CUT TO: Bob Kerry Ltd. Morning.
JACK is sitting at his father's desk, quickly going through the drawers, obviously searching for something. He still wears his outdoor clothes, and his manner is tense and agitated. LIZ stands watching him.

LIZ: I don't know anything about it, Mr Kerry. I don't remember the file …

JACK: Douglas had it. It was my father's … It's just an ordinary blue folder, but there was a number scribbled on it – a car number …

LIZ: A car number?

JACK: Yes … 384 JKY … At least I think that was it … I want to make certain …

LIZ shakes her head, puzzled. DOUGLAS comes up the spiral staircase, from the basement, carrying a new golf bag and several boxes of tennis balls.

JACK: (*Turning*) Douglas, you remember that folder you had on Monday morning, my father's …?

DOUGLAS: Yes.

JACK: Where is it?

DOUGLAS looks at JACK, surprised by the urgency in his voice. He hands LIZ the things he is carrying and crosses to his desk. LIZ hesitates, then returns to the shop. DOUGLAS takes the folder out of a drawer and gives it to JACK, who immediately looks at the cover.

JACK: (*Quietly*) I knew damn well I was right! (*To DOUGLAS; looking up*) This number … 384 JKY … you asked my father about it.

20

DOUGLAS: Yes, I didn't know what it was. I thought he'd made a note of it for some reason or other ... He said he hadn't but I'm sure it's his handwriting.

JACK: I saw the number this morning ... on a Fiat estate car. Delaney was driving it.

DOUGLAS: (*Surprised*) Delaney?

JACK: Yes.

DOUGLAS: Are you sure, Jack?

JACK: I'm absolutely sure.

JACK stands for a moment, deep in thought, looking at the folder. Suddenly, he puts it down on the phone and picks up a telephone directory. He starts searching for DELANEY's phone number.

CUT TO: A White Telephone on an ornate bedroom table.
The telephone starts ringing. RUPERT DELANEY appears and lifts the receiver.

RUPERT: Knightsbridge 1872 ...

CUT TO:

JACK: (*On the phone*) Rupert Delaney?

CUT TO:

RUPERT: (*Hesitating*) Yes ...

CUT TO:

JACK: This is Jack Kerry ...

CUT TO:

RUPERT: (*Nervously*) I'm – I'm sorry I missed you at the inquest, Mr Kerry. I just wanted to say once again, how very sorry I am about everything.

CUT TO:
JACK: (*Briskly; interrupting RUPERT*) I'd like to see you, Delaney. When can we meet? Tonight?

CUT TO:
RUPERT: Well – I have a dinner date, but I expect I'll be back by about half past ten.

CUT TO:
JACK: I'll see you then. (*Looking at the phone book on the desk*) 3, Linton Close, Knightsbridge …

CUT TO:
RUPERT: Yes, it's rather difficult to find, Mr Kerry. It's in a mews just off Kennerton Street.

CUT TO:
JACK: Don't worry, I'll find it.

CUT TO:
RUPERT: Come straight up – I'm on the first floor.

CUT TO:
JACK: Right. Half past ten.
JACK replaces the receiver and turns from the desk. DOUGLAS is watching him; curious.

CUT TO: Linton Close, Knightsbridge. Night.
This is a large, secluded mews with several garages, and two or three houses converted into flats. The mews is well lit but deserted – except for DELANEY's estate car which is parked opposite the entrance to one of the lock-up garages.
JACK's Austin turns out of Kennerton Street and enters the mews, stopping about twenty yards or so away from the estate

22

car. JACK gets out of the Austin and, after looking at the flat –
his eyes resting for a second or two on the registration number
– he turns and walks towards one of the houses. He looks at the
large brass three on the door of the house. The door is ajar –
after a momentary hesitation he pushes the door open and goes
inside.

CUT TO: Inside the house. Night.
JACK emerges from a narrow staircase to find himself facing
the ornate front door of RUPERT DELANEY's flat.
DELANEY's visiting card, framed, is displayed by the bell
push. Jack rings the bell.
A pause.
We hear the chimes, but there is no answer. Jack rings again.
No answer. He rings the bell for a third time – still no answer.
JACK hesitates, as if to turn away and then looks at his watch.
Suddenly, inside the flat, the telephone starts to ring, and JACK
looks up. He stands listening to the telephone ringing – after a
while it stops, unanswered. JACK turns and crosses to the
staircase.

CUT TO: Linton Close, Knightsbridge. Night.
JACK comes out of the front door of the house and walks
towards his car. Just before he reaches the Austin, he looks
across at the estate car and something catches his eye. He
hesitates; stands looking at the flat for a moment, then slowly
strolls across to it. We see now what has aroused his curiosity
– a scarf is on the ground, near the rear passenger door. It
looks as if it has fallen out of the car. JACK picks up the scarf
and looks at it; it is a girl's flimsy, colourful headscarf. As
JACK examines the scarf a sudden thought occurs to him, and
he quickly turns, and snatches open the car door.
The Fiat is empty. We see an open packet of cigarettes on the
front seat, and an evening newspaper. JACK stands for a

second, then he throws the scarf down beside the newspaper and, closing the door, returns to his own car.

JACK reaches his car and, deep in thought, is just about to open the door when he stops in his tracks. We see RUPERT DELANEY – mouth open, eyes staring. His body is slumped across the two front seats of the Austin.

CUT TO: Linton Close, Knightsbridge. Twenty minutes later. *The mews is no longer deserted. Local police, Scotland Yard officials, newspaper reporters etc can be seen milling around. A police ambulance is standing next to the Austin, and DELANEY's body is about to be transferred to it.*

ED ROYCE is leaning against the Fiat, talking to a colleague; one of the fingerprint men. JACK is sitting in a stationary police car next to CHIEF SUPERINTENDENT HAL BROMFORD.

CUT TO: Inside the Police Car.
JACK looks tense and worried. The SUPERINTENDENT is a big man; fully aware of his height and authority.

BROMFORD: … This girl – the girl you saw with Delaney this morning – would you recognise her again?

JACK: Yes, I would.

BROMFORD: Okay. Go on, Kerry …

JACK: Well – as soon as I realised that the car number was the same, I telephoned Delaney and made an appointment to see him.

BROMFORD: Why?

JACK: I wanted to question him. I wanted to find out … (*He hesitates*)

BROMFORD: Find out what?

JACK: It's my belief – my firm belief – that Delaney knew my father. (*Shaking his head*) I don't think my father was killed accidentally, sir.

24

BROMFORD: I don't know about your father, Delaney certainly wasn't. He was shot through the back of his head. (*He looks at JACK*) Kerry, you didn't like Rupert Delaney, did you?

JACK: (*Irritated*) It wasn't a question of not liking him. I didn't know the man.

BROMFORD: You knew him well enough to phone him and make an appointment to see him this evening.

ED approaches.

JACK: I've told you why I made that appointment! I was curious. It seemed very odd to me that my father should have written down the number of Delaney's car when ... (*He stops, seeing ED at the car window*)

BROMFORD: Yes – what is it, Ed?

ED: There's no sign of the gun – it might be in the mews, but we've searched it pretty thoroughly. We're going up to the flat now.

BROMFORD: Okay.

ED looks at JACK, hesitates, then hands the SUPERINTENDENT a slip of paper.

ED: We found this on Delaney, sir, it was in his waistcoat pocket.

BROMFORD looks at ED, then takes the slip of paper from him and glances at it. ED moves away. BROMFORD, after a slight pause, looks at JACK.

BROMFORD: When you spoke to Delaney on the phone did he say anything about a letter?

JACK: A letter?

BROMFORD: Yes.

JACK: (*Shaking his head*) No. Why should he?

BROMFORD: Apparently, he sent you a letter, a registered letter. He posted it today. Here's the receipt.

Puzzled, JACK takes the receipt from BROMFORD and looks at it.

BROMFORD: Have you any idea what was in that letter, what he wrote to you about?

JACK: No – not the slightest.

BROMFORD: You're sure?

JACK: Of course, I'm sure!

BROMFORD: Well, don't worry, you'll know tomorrow morning, Kerry. We'll both know.

CUT TO: The Living Room of the Flat. Morning.

JACK enters from the bedroom; he is wearing a dressing-gown over his pyjamas and looks as if he has had very little sleep during the night. He crosses out into the hall, and, opening the front door, picks up a copy of the morning newspaper. JACK is looking at a photograph of RUPERT DELANEY on the front page of the newspaper when the SUPERINTENDENT appears at the head of the stairs. JACK is surprised to see him.

JACK: Good morning.

BROMFORD: Am I too early for you?

JACK: No; come along in.

BROMFORD: Has the post been?

JACK: Not yet. (*He looks at his watch*) It should be here any minute.

BROMFORD enters the hall and JACK closes the front door. BROMFORD and JACK enter the living room.

JACK: Would you like some coffee? I was just going to make some.

BROMFORD: Not for me – but you go ahead.

JACK: There was no need to call round, sir – I'd have delivered the letter to you.

BROMFORD: Yes, I know that. But I wanted to see you. (*Indicating the armchair*) May I sit down?

JACK: Yes, of course.

26

BROMFORD sits in the armchair and takes stock of his surroundings. JACK crosses to the arm of the settee.

BROMFORD: Go ahead – make your coffee.

JACK: That's all right. The coffee can wait. I've plenty of time, I'm on leave anyway.

BROMFORD: Ah, yes – until when?

JACK: The twenty-fifth. What is it you wanted to see me about?

BROMFORD looks at JACK for a moment.

BROMFORD: Kerry, you told me last night that you'd never met Delaney, not until you saw him at the golf club.

JACK: That's right.

BROMFORD: You saw him at the club the morning your father was killed, and at the Inquest.

JACK: Yes.

BROMFORD: Did you speak to him at the Inquest?

JACK: No.

BROMFORD: Why not?

JACK: I didn't feel particularly friendly towards him.

BROMFORD: (*Nodding*) Yes, I can understand that.

JACK: Besides, I … knew precisely what was going to happen at the Inquest. I felt angry – damned angry about the whole business.

BROMFORD: Yes, that's what Ed Royce told me. (*A moment, then suddenly:*) Tell me: do you know a man called Higgs?

JACK: (*Surprised by the question*) Higgs? No – I don't think so.

BROMFORD takes his wallet out of his pocket.

BROMFORD: Basil Higgs …

JACK: Basil … (*He rises*) I made a cheque out to a man called Basil Higgs yesterday morning.

BROMFORD: That's right you did. (*He produces the cheque from the wallet*) You did indeed, Kerry. (*Showing the cheque to JACK*) For five pounds.

JACK: But where did you get that cheque?

BROMFORD: We found it, last night.

JACK: Where?

BROMFORD: In a drawer in Rupert Delaney's flat.

JACK: But – I didn't give it to Delaney.

BROMFORD: I'm quite prepared to believe that, since it's made out to a Mr Higgs.

JACK: Yes, but I didn't give it to Higgs either. You see I … Look, let me explain.

BROMFORD: Go ahead.

JACK: My housekeeper, Mrs Lincoln, lost a poodle. We advertised for it and offered a reward. Some people called Bannister, in Hampstead, found the poodle and I drove over there yesterday morning and picked it up. When I was leaving, I mentioned the reward, and Charles Bannister suggested that I give the fiver to a pet charity of his. He asked me to make the cheque out to the Secretary – (*Pointing to the cheque*) Basil Higgs.

BROMFORD: I see. Then how did Delaney get hold of it?

JACK: (*Puzzled*) I don't know. I just can't imagine.

BROMFORD looks at JACK, then at the cheque again – as he does so the door bell rings. JACK turns towards the hall.

BROMFORD: Is that the post?

JACK: Most probably.

As BROMFORD rises, JACK goes out into the hall and opens the front door. A POSTMAN stands in the doorway, several letters in his hand, including a long, bulky envelope.

POSTMAN: Good morning.

JACK: Good morning.

POSTMAN: There's a registered letter, sir. Sign here, please.

JACK signs the slip and takes the letters.

JACK: Thank you.

JACK closes the door and stands looking at the letters. He slowly enters the living room. He is still looking at the long envelope.

BROMFORD: Has it arrived?

JACK: Yes.

JACK crosses to the desk, picks up the letter opener, and slits open the long envelope. BROMFORD moves down to him, almost unable to contain his curiosity. JACK takes a single sheet of notepaper out of the envelope.

BROMFORD: What does the note say?

The camera zooms in on the handwritten note in JACK's hand. It is a plain piece of notepaper with no date or address on it. The note reads: "This is why your father was killed. Rupert Delany". JACK and BROMFORD stare at the note.

BROMFORD: (*Puzzled*) This is why your father was killed?

JACK looks down at the envelope again, then he tears it completely open and takes out an object carefully wrapped in tissue paper. He disposes of the tissue paper, revealing an ornate, beautifully made dog collar.

JACK: It's the collar!

BROMFORD: The collar?

JACK: (*Astonished*) Yes – the one that was stolen! The one Midge was wearing!

END OF EPISODE ONE

EPISODE TWO

OPEN TO: The Living Room of Jack Kerry's Flat. Morning.
JACK is looking at the dog collar which he is holding in his hand. A puzzled SUPERINTENDENT BROMFORD is staring at JACK.

BROMFORD: What do you mean, it's the one that was stolen – the one Midge was wearing?

JACK: I told you. My housekeeper lost her poodle and we advertised for it. Some people called Bannister found ...

BROMFORD: Now wait a minute! (*He points to the collar*) You're sure this is the collar – the one that was on the poodle?

JACK: Yes, I'm sure.

BROMFORD: (*Puzzled*) Then what the devil does the note mean – "This is why your father was killed"?

JACK: I don't know – I can't imagine.

BROMFORD: (*Suddenly*) All right, Kerry – start at the beginning, tell me the whole story.

JACK: But I've already told you ...

BROMFORD: Tell me again!

JACK: (*After a moment*) Mrs Lincoln, my housekeeper, has a poodle – Midge. It disappeared and we advertised for it in the local newspaper. Yesterday morning, a woman called Mrs Bannister phoned me and said that she'd found the dog. I drove out to her house – a house called Stillwater in Lawrence Avenue, Hampstead. The dog was all right except that its collar was missing.

BROMFORD: What time was this?

JACK: Oh – about twelve fifteen ...

BROMFORD: Go on.

JACK: Just as I was leaving, I mentioned the fact that we'd offered a reward and Charles Bannister –

	that's the husband – suggested I gave the fiver to a local charity. At Bannister's request, I made the cheque payable to the Secretary – someone called Basil Higgs.
BROMFORD:	I see. (*Looking at JACK*) I take it you'd never met the Bannisters before?
JACK:	No. Never. I'd never heard of them. They seemed very nice people. He's an invalid; he was in a wheelchair.
BROMFORD:	Right; now tell me about the collar. Where did it come from originally?
JACK:	I don't know where it came from. All I know is my father gave it to Mrs Lincoln for her birthday.
BROMFORD:	When was this?
JACK:	About a month ago. Unfortunately Mrs Lincoln's away at the moment, her nephew got the flu and she's looking after him for a few days. (*A sudden thought*) But wait a minute! I wonder if Liz can help us?
BROMFORD:	Liz?
JACK:	Liz Mason. She works in the shop.
BROMFORD:	How can she help us?
JACK:	My father hadn't the slightest idea what to buy Mrs Lincoln, so he consulted Liz about it.
BROMFORD:	And she suggested a collar, for the poodle?
JACK:	Yes – at least, I think she did.

BROMFORD hesitates, then makes a decision.

BROMFORD:	All right, Kerry – talk to her about it. Show her the collar, see what she says, ask her if she knows where your father got it from.
JACK:	(*Thoughtfully looking at the dog collar*) What the devil was Delaney getting at? I just can't imagine what he meant.

BROMFORD: Neither can I. It looks a perfectly ordinary collar to me – a little ornate perhaps. (*He rises*) I'd like to see you later this morning. Could you be in my office about eleven o'clock?

The door bell rings.

JACK: Yes, I shall be in the building. They're taking my prints some time this morning.

BROMFORD: (*Casually*) It's routine – they're giving your car another going over.

JACK looks at the SUPERINTENDENT then goes out into the hall and opens the front door. ED is in the doorway, finger on the bell push – he carries a large folder.

ED: Hello, Jack? Is Bromford here?

JACK: He is – he is indeed. Come along in, Ed.

ED enters the living room followed by JACK. The SUPERINTENDENT is obviously surprised to see him.

BROMFORD: Hello, Ed …

ED: Good morning, sir. I've just come from Delaney's place. Things are beginning to get interesting, sir.

JACK: Would you like some coffee, Ed?

ED: No, thank you.

BROMFORD: What do you mean – interesting?

ED: We were just leaving the flat when Jackson found a door behind what we thought was a larder. There was a small room, fitted up as an office. Desk, typewriter, filing cabinet, usual office paraphernalia.

BROMFORD: Well?

ED: (*Moving to the table*) We've just spent a fascinating half hour going through the filing cabinet, sir – to say nothing of the desk.

BROMFORD: Get to the point.

JACK: (*Quietly*) What did you find, Ed?

ED looks at JACK, then at the SUPERINTENDENT. Suddenly, he opens the folder and spills about twenty-five postcard size photographs onto the table, photos of girls. Nudes: semi-nudes: photographs taken at Soho strip clubs; head and shoulders photographs; girls in bikinis. JACK picks up one of the photos and looks at it.

JACK: I know this girl. She's a prostitute – she gave evidence in the Oxford case about six months ago.

ED: (*He nods and indicates the photos on the table*) It's my guess they're all prostitutes – every one of them. (*To BROMFORD*) There's over two hundred photos in that room, sir.

BROMFORD: (*Surprised*) Two hundred?

ED: That's right. No names, no phone numbers, no addresses, no details of any kind. Just the photographs.

BROMFORD looks at ED, obviously puzzled. He picks up one of the photos from the table.

BROMFORD: (*Quietly*) What the hell was Delaney up to?

CUT TO: Bob Kerry Ltd. Morning.

LIZ is examining the collar. She is standing next to JACK in the office.

LIZ: It certainly looks like the same collar. But where did you get it from, Mr Kerry? I thought you said that Midge wasn't wearing a collar when he was found.

JACK: (*Interrupting LIZ*) Don't worry your head about that, Liz. All I want to know is – is it the same collar? Is it the one my father bought?

LIZ: Yes ... (*Examining the collar again*) The medallion looks a little different, but ...

JACK: What do you mean, it looks different?

36

JACK takes the collar from LIZ.

LIZ: I thought the medallion seemed a little bit smaller, but ... (*Shaking her head*) No, it's the same collar, I'm sure of it.

JACK: Have you any idea where my father bought it?

LIZ: Yes, he bought it from Penn's pet shop.

JACK: Where's that?

LIZ: It's in St John's Wood; I think it's Valence Road.

JACK: Did you send him there?

LIZ: No, I didn't. We were talking about Mrs Lincoln one morning and your father said he didn't know what on earth to buy her for her birthday. One of us suggested a collar for Midge – I don't know who it was – and Douglas said there was only one place to buy a dog collar and that was Penn's pet shop.

JACK: I see. (*Dismissing LIZ*) Thank you. (*Suddenly*) Oh, Liz, there's something I've been meaning to ask you.

LIZ: Yes, Mr Kerry?

JACK: You saw a great deal of my father; you saw him most days in fact. Did he ever say anything – or do anything that ... well, aroused your curiosity at all?

LIZ hesitates, is about to say something, then changes her mind.

LIZ: No, I don't think so.

JACK: Are you sure?

LIZ: Well ... (*Still hesitating*) ... There was one incident, but it was nothing, it really wasn't anything important.

JACK: Tell me about it, Liz.

LIZ: One day last week, I think it was Tuesday, I arrived back from lunch and your father was talking to a customer – at least I assumed she was a customer.

37

JACK: She?

LIZ: Yes – a tall, dark, good-looking woman of about fifty; very smartly dressed. When I entered the shop, I heard your father say, "For God's sake, Iris, don't be difficult about ..." And then suddenly he saw me and started talking about something quite different.

JACK: Go on.

LIZ: That's all. I came in here, a few minutes later the woman left.

JACK: Did my father mention her at all – make any comment?

LIZ: Yes, he made a point of telling me that he'd never seen her before. He said she was looking for a special kind of ski jacket.

JACK: Did you believe him?

LIZ: I – I didn't know whether to believe him or not. It certainly sounded convincing.

JACK: Did you tell Douglas about this?

LIZ: No, I didn't tell anyone about it. It didn't seem to me to be important. In any case, it was none of my business.

JACK: (*Nodding*) Thank you, Liz.

LIZ gives JACK a little smile – then goes out of the office. JACK stands by the desk, deep in thought. After a moment, almost without realising what he is doing, he picks up the collar again.

CUT TO: NORMAN PENN's Pet Shop, St John's Wood, London. Morning.

This is a tiny shop specialising in almost everything connected with household pets. Several pets are on display, including white mice, rabbits, puppies, birds in cages, etc. On a stand in the centre of the shop can be seen a display of dog collars and tailor-made jackets for the more sophisticated animal. At the rear of the shop a curtain leads to an office-cum-private den.

NORMAN PENN is tidying up the shop when JACK enters, carrying Midge's collar. PENN is a heavily built man with spectacles, crinkly hair, and a somewhat disarming manner.

JACK: Good morning.

PENN: Good morning, sir.

JACK: Mr Penn?

PENN: Yes – what can I do for you, sir?

JACK: I'm a police officer, Mr Penn – from Scotland Yard – and I'm making a few inquiries. I think perhaps you might be able to help me.

PENN: Well, if I can, I will certainly, my dear sir.

PENN moves towards JACK; he is curious and looks at the dog collar in JACK's hand.

PENN: What is it you're making inquiries about?

JACK: About this collar. I understand my father – Bob Kerry – bought it from you about …

PENN: (*Surprised; interrupting JACK*) Are you Mr Kerry's son?

JACK: Yes …

PENN: Oh, Mr Kerry, I'm delighted to meet you! But I was so distressed to read about your father! What a dreadful thing to have happened!

JACK: Thank you, Mr Penn. Did you know my father?

PENN: No – but we met, of course, when he bought the collar. I'd been an admirer of his for years. I was very thrilled when he came into my shop that afternoon. You'll find it hard to believe, Mr Kerry, but I was quite an athlete myself in the old days.

JACK: Mr Penn, I want you to take a look at this collar and tell me; first of all, whether it's the one you sold my father, and secondly whether there's anything unusual about it.

PENN takes the collar and examines it. Then he looks at JACK obviously puzzled.

PENN: Yes, this is the collar your father bought, so far as I can tell …

JACK: So far as you can tell?

PENN: (*Smiling*) Well – I've sold quite a few like this, and they all look very much alike, of course. (*Indicating the display stand*) As you see, I've quite a stock on hand at the moment.

PENN picks up a collar from the stand.

PENN: Some are a little more decorative than others perhaps, but they're all more or less the same. (*He looks at Midge's collar again*) I don't think there's anything unusual about this one, Mr Kerry.

JACK: (*Pointing to the collar*) What about the medallion – is that the same one, or has it been changed?

PENN: It looks exactly the same to me – but you realise, of course, I didn't supply this particular medallion. Your father brought it with him.

JACK looks at PENN and takes the collar from him.

JACK: He brought it with him?

PENN: Yes. (*Suddenly remembering*) No! No, I'm terribly sorry! I've just remembered, his friend brought it. That's right – your father was trying to make up his mind whether to buy the collar or not, and then his friend arrived. She said it was absolutely perfect and just the very thing he wanted.

JACK: And she had the medallion?

PENN: That's right. She took it out of her handbag, and I fitted it on to the collar. They were both highly delighted with it.

JACK: (*Pointing to the medallion*) Was the name and address already on the medallion, or did you put it on?

40

PENN: No, no, it was already on.

JACK: (*After a moment; quietly*) Who was this friend of my father's, do you know?

PENN: No, I'm afraid I don't. She seemed a very charming lady.

JACK: About fifty; tall, dark, very well dressed?

PENN: Yes, she was wearing one of those lovely fur coats – what do you call them? Ocelot? Yes, that's right, Ocelot.

JACK looks at the collar again, his thoughts elsewhere – suddenly he gives PENN a friendly nod and moves towards the door.

JACK: Thank you, Mr Penn – you've been most helpful.

PENN: (*Puzzled but friendly*) Thank you, sir. (*Opening the shop door*) I do hope we shall meet again, Mr Kerry.

CUT TO: CHIEF SUPERINTENDENT BROMFORD's Office at Scotland Yard. Morning.

BROMFORD's office is large and spacious with a window looking out towards the Embankment. There is a large partner's desk and several comfortable chairs. The walls are bare except for one rather complicated looking chart and a reproduction of a Bernard Buffet painting of London. There is a small secretarial office on the right of the door which leads out into the corridor.

A uniformed clerk, HODGES, enters from the corridor, followed by JACK.

HODGES: The Superintendent hasn't returned from Hampstead yet, sir.

JACK: (*Curious*) Hampstead?

HODGES: Yes, sir. He went out there first thing this morning.

JACK: All right, Hodges, I'll wait.

HODGES: I think Inspector Royce is in the other office, sir.

41

AS HODGES crosses towards the other office, ED comes out of it carrying a snapshot photograph in his hand. He is obviously pleased to see JACK.

ED: Jack, I've been trying to get hold of you! You're just the man I want to see!

JACK: What is it, Ed?

HODGES goes into the other office.

ED: (*Offering JACK the snapshot*) Take a look at this.

JACK puts the collar he is carrying on the desk and takes the photograph. The photo is obviously a holiday snapshot, showing RUPERT DELANEY and CATHY WHITE sunbathing by the side of the pool. JACK looks at the photo.

ED: Do you recognise her?

JACK: (*Looking up*) Yes, she's the girl that was with Delaney, the girl I told you about, the girl he was having a row with in the car.

ED nods and takes the photograph from JACK.

ED: I was hoping you'd say that.

JACK: But who is she?

ED: Her name's Cathy White. She's been living with Delaney. Last night they had dinner together at a place in Charlotte Street. Apparently, they had a flaming row and left the restaurant together at about half past nine.

JACK: (*Quickly*) Have you picked her up?

ED: Not yet.

JACK: (*Angrily*) Why not, for Pete's sake?

ED: Why not? My God, you sound just like Bromford! Because we can't find her, Jack, that's why not!

JACK: Did she go back to the flat with Delaney?

ED: We don't know – that's what we're trying to find out.

JACK: Where's this girl come from? What's her background?

ED: She's from Liverpool; apparently Delaney saw her in a show up there and persuaded her to come to town. She was in one musical – the one at the St Edward's – and it flopped. Until about a month ago she was in digs at Notting Hill Gate, then she moved in with Delaney.

JACK: Who told you all this?

ED: Her ex-landlady.

JACK: And what about Delaney?

ED: We're not making any headway, I'm afraid. No one wants to talk about him. All we've learnt so far is that he had a private income and backed one or two shows in the West End, including the flop Cathy was in. Anyway, I've told Sergeant Quilter to snoop around, he usually comes up with something.

JACK: Ed, whatever happens you've got to find that girl.

ED: Don't worry, I'll find her.

The door opens and BROMFORD enters.

BROMFORD: (*To JACK*) Sorry to have kept you, I've been out to Hampstead. (*To ED*) Any news? Have you picked the girl up yet?

ED: No, not yet, sir. (*Indicating the snapshot*) But Jack's identified her, she was the girl in the car. And the landlady now thinks …

BROMFORD: (*Curtly crossing to the desk*) I don't want to hear any more about the landlady! I want that girl. Cathy White! Find her. (*He sits at his desk*) Sit down, Kerry.

JACK hesitates, looks at ED, then sits in one of the armchairs.

ED: We'll be finished with your car by three o'clock, Jack, if you'd like to pick it up.

JACK: Thank you, Ed.

ED: (*To BROMFORD*) I'll be in my office if you want me, sir.

ED goes out. The SUPERINTENDENT looks at JACK, picks up a report on his desk, and glances at it.

BROMFORD: (*Still looking at the report*) I've seen the Bannisters this morning.

JACK: Yes, I thought perhaps you had.

BROMFORD: They confirm your story, about the dog.

JACK: I'm pleased to hear it. What did you expect?

BROMFORD looks up. He hesitates, there is obviously something on his mind.

BROMFORD: Kerry, I think perhaps I'd better tell you what happened this morning. (*He puts down the report*) I arrived at the house about a quarter past nine. There was a Bentley on the drive, and a rather good-looking woman was standing near the open boot of the car. I knew, from what you'd told me, she was Mrs Bannister.

CUT TO: The Drive of Stillwater, CHARLES BANNISTER's house at Hampstead, London. Morning.

A police car turns through the gate and into the drive. As it does so, IRIS BANNISTER, who is standing near a continental BENTLEY, is obviously surprised. She is wearing an ocelot coat and is dressed for a journey. The SUPERINTENDENT climbs out of the car, says something to the uniformed driver, then crosses towards IRIS. He takes off his hat as he approaches her.

BROMFORD: (*Pleasantly*) Mrs Bannister?

IRIS: Yes?

BROMFORD: Good morning, Mrs Bannister. I'm from Scotland Yard, Superintendent Bromford. I'd be very grateful if you could spare me a moment.

IRIS: (*Pleasantly*) Yes, of course – but, I'm afraid it will only have to be a moment, Superintendent. My husband and I are leaving for Aldeburgh, and we're late already, I'm afraid.

BROMFORD: Don't worry, madam – I won't detain you. I'm simply making inquiries on behalf of a friend of mine, Jack Kerry.

IRIS: (*Surprised*) Mr Kerry?

BROMFORD: Yes, I think you saw Mr Kerry yesterday afternoon?

IRIS: That's right, we did. My husband found Mr Kerry's dog or rather his housekeeper's and I telephoned him. He came out here just before lunch.

BROMFORD: (*Nodding*) Yes – so I understand. I also understand he gave your husband a cheque.

IRIS: A cheque?

BROMFORD: Yes – for five pounds.

IRIS: (*Puzzled*) I think you're mistaken, Superintendent. But here's my husband now, perhaps you'll have a word with him.

The SUPERINTENDENT turns and looks towards the house. CHARLES BANNISTER emerges from the house and walks towards the Bentley. He is carrying a suitcase and looks particularly fit and well. He is dressed precisely the same as when we last saw him in the wheelchair. It is obvious he is a little puzzled by the presence of BROMFORD and the police car.

IRIS: (*As her husband approaches*) Charles, this is Superintendent Bromford, he's from Scotland Yard.

The SUPERINTENDENT stares at BANNISTER with obvious interest as he puts the suitcase down on the drive.

BANNISTER: Good morning, Superintendent! What can I do for you?

BROMFORD: I'm making inquiries about a cheque, sir. The one Mr Kerry gave you.

BANNISTER: (*Also puzzled*) The one Mr Kerry gave me? Aren't you mistaken? I don't know anything about a cheque. Mr Kerry came out here to collect a poodle.

BROMFORD: Yes, I know, sir, but would you mind telling me what happened yesterday afternoon, Mr Bannister?

BANNISTER: What happened?

BROMFORD: Between you and Mr Kerry?

BANNISTER: (*A shrug*) Nothing happened. He simply collected the poodle, and we had a little natter about the fact that the dog's collar was missing – and, well … that was it. I don't suppose he was with us more than five minutes.

BROMFORD: I see.

BANNISTER looks at IRIS.

IRIS: That's true, Superintendent.

BANNISTER: Look, what is this, old man? What's it all about?

BROMFORD: I'm sorry, sir, I've obviously been under a misapprehension. I thought Kerry gave you a cheque – made out to someone called Higgs.

BANNISTER: Why on earth should he do that? (*Amused*) Higgs, did you say?

BROMFORD: Yes, Basil Higgs.

BANNISTER: I've never heard of anyone called Basil Higgs.

BROMFORD: Have you heard of an organisation – a local one, I believe, called the Hamsters?

BANNISTER: The Hamsters? No – no, I haven't. Have you, Iris?

IRIS: (*With a little laugh*) No, I'm afraid I haven't.

BROMFORD: (*Quickly*) Well – thank you, Mr Bannister. I'm sorry to have troubled you. (*He turns, hesitates – apparently an afterthought*) Oh, there is one other thing, I do hope you won't mind my asking, sir.

BANNISTER: No – go ahead …

BROMFORD: Well – er – when you saw Mr Kerry yesterday afternoon were you, by any chance, for some reason or other … in a wheelchair?

BANNISTER: (*Staggered*) In a wheelchair?

BROMFORD: Yes.

IRIS: You mean – an invalid chair?

BROMFORD: Yes, Mrs Bannister.

BANNISTER: Good God, no! Why should I be in a wheelchair? I know I look pretty senile, old boy – but I haven't quite reached the bathchair stage, not yet. (*To IRIS*) Have I, Iris?

IRIS: Not yet, sweetie.

BROMFORD: (*Smiles*) Thank you, sir – Mrs Bannister – you've been very helpful. I hope you have a pleasant journey.

BROMFORD nods to CHARLES and IRIS and returns to the police car. The BANNISTERs stand watching him, both apparently very bewildered. We hear BROMFORD's voice as the camera pans the police car out of the drive and into the avenue.

BROMFORD: (*Out of vision*) After I'd seen the Bannisters, I dropped in on an old friend of mine – Inspector Everson. He knows Hampstead better than you know your flat, Kerry – he should, he's been there for over twenty years.

CUT TO: CHIEF SUPERINTENDENT BROMFORD's Office at Scotland Yard. Morning.

JACK is listening to the SUPERINTENDENT who is still sitting behind the desk facing him.

BROMFORD: I questioned the Inspector about the Bannisters and he said that Charles Bannister was a retired stockbroker. He bought Stillwater in 1963 and paid over thirty thousand for it. I also mentioned the wheelchair. (*Shaking his head*) Bannister's as fit as a fiddle: he plays squash twice a week and golf on Sundays.

JACK rises and moves to the desk.

JACK: (*Bewildered and angry*) I don't care whether he plays tennis, golf, squash, or anything else – he was in a wheelchair when I saw him yesterday afternoon! Good God, why should I say a thing like that, if it wasn't true?

BROMFORD: (*Quietly*) I can't imagine why.

JACK: (*Looking at BROMFORD*) You don't believe me, do you?

BROMFORD doesn't answer, instead he picks up the collar and looks at it.

BROMFORD: (*After a moment*) Tell me about the collar – did you find out anything?

JACK: (*Just managing to control his anger*) It was bought by my father from a shop in St. John's Wood. There's a doubt – a slight doubt – about the medallion.

ROMFORD looks at the medallion.

BROMFORD: You mean – it might have been changed?

JACK: Yes.

BROMFORD: It's got Mrs Lincoln's name on it and your phone number.

There is a knock on the door.

48

JACK: Yes, but both Liz Mason and the man in the pet shop, a man called Penn, were a little doubtful about it.

The door opens. Ed is in the doorway.

ED: (*To BROMFORD*) Can you spare a moment, sir?

BROMFORD: Yes, what it is, Ed?

ED enters the office.

ED: I've just had a call from Sergeant Quilter. He's found out something about Delaney, sir – something we didn't know.

BROMFORD: Well?

ED: His name wasn't Rupert Delaney, that's just a name he used because he disliked his own so much. (*He stares across at Jack and moves towards the desk*) His real name was Higgs, sir – Basil Higgs.

The SUPERINTENDENT rises from his desk.

CUT TO: Outside Bob Kerry Ltd. Late Afternoon.

There is an empty taxi parked near the kerb. JACK drives up in the Austin 1100. And as he climbs out of the car DOUGLAS emerges from the shop. He is on his way home and locks the door of the shop then, turning, suddenly sees JACK.

JACK: Hello, Doug! Just leaving?

DOUGLAS: Oh, hello, Jack! Yes, I'm just off.

JACK: What sort of a day has it been?

DOUGLAS: It's been pretty good. I was surprised – it was quiet this morning and then suddenly at about half past three we were rushed off our feet. (*Suddenly, remembering*) By the way – who do you think phoned this morning, just after you left? Your housekeeper's nephew, Leonard Lincoln.

JACK:	Leonard Lincoln?
DOUGLAS:	Yes, the extraordinary thing is he wanted to talk to his aunt. He said he'd tried your flat several times and since there was no reply, he thought …
JACK:	(*Surprised*) But I thought he had the flu and Mrs Lincoln was looking after him?
DOUGLAS:	Yes, I know, that's what I thought – that's what I told him. But apparently it wasn't true.
JACK:	What did he say?
DOUGLAS:	The poor man was embarrassed – he didn't know what to say. Do you think she's walked out on you, Jack?
JACK:	Well – it's beginning to sound like it.
DOUGLAS:	Incidentally, I told him Midge was back – he said he'd tell his aunt when she got in touch with him.

JACK nods, his thoughts obviously elsewhere.

DOUGLAS:	Is there any news, Jack?
JACK:	News?
DOUGLAS:	About the Delaney murder?
JACK:	Oh, yes – we're looking for a girl called Cathy White.
DOUGLAS:	Is that the girl you told me about – the one you saw in the car?
JACK:	Yes, she and Delaney had dinner together last night.
DOUGLAS:	Do you think she did it?
JACK:	(*His thoughts still on MRS LINCOLN*) Did what?
DOUGLAS:	The murder? …
JACK:	Good God, Douglas, ask me another! Your guess is as good as mine!

DOUGLAS: Yes, but – could she have done it? Could a woman have committed the murder?

JACK: Yes, of course – why not? He was shot. He wasn't strangled or anything like that. (*Suddenly patting DOUGLAS on the arm*) See you tomorrow, Doug.

DOUGLAS: Good night, Jack.

JACK: Good night.

JACK crosses towards the entrance to his flat – as he reaches the door it suddenly opens and WALLY STONE, a taxi driver, comes out, carrying two suitcases and a dilapidated hatbox. WALLY nods to JACK and crosses to his cab. JACK stares at him for a second or two, then goes into the building.

CUT TO: The Entrance Hall to JACK KERRY's Flat. Late Afternoon.

This is a small entrance hall with a staircase leading up to the front door of the flat.

JACK comes into the hall from the street as FREDA LINCOLN comes down the staircase carrying Midge. At first, she doesn't see JACK, she is too busy fondling the poodle; talking to it. Suddenly, she looks up and to her surprise and embarrassment finds JACK, at the foot of the staircase, watching her.

JACK: Good evening, Mrs Lincoln.

FREDA: Oh! Oh, hello, Mr Kerry. (*Forcing a smile*) I – I was hoping to see you.

JACK: Were you, Mrs Lincoln? I find that a little difficult to believe. I trust your nephew's fully recovered from the flu by now?

FREDA has now reached the hall.

FREDA: Oh, yes, Mr Kerry, thank you, he's … (*Seeing JACK's expression*) Mr Kerry, I'm afraid I owe you an apology. I lied to you about Leonard. To cut a long story short, I've …

51

JACK: You've got another job, Mrs Lincoln?

FREDA: (*Relieved*) Yes, I have. I've taken a job at that new hotel in Knightsbridge – the Royal Plaza.

JACK: Well, why on earth didn't you tell me about it?

FREDA: (*Flustered*) I just didn't know what to do. After your father died, I … I … Well, I just couldn't settle, Mr Kerry. I'm sorry – very sorry – you've always been kind to me, and I don't want to appear ungrateful, but …

JACK: Mrs Lincoln, you were quite at liberty to take another job – in fact, I rather thought you would. But surely there was no need …

FREDA: (*On the verge of taking offence*) I've told you, I apologise, Mr Kerry. I behaved badly, and I'm really sorry about it.

JACK: (*He looks at FREDA; after a moment:*) Do I owe you any money?

FREDA: No, no, we're all square, thank you, sir.

JACK touches the poodle, but looks at FREDA.

JACK: Well – anyway, we found Midge for you.

FREDA: Yes; and you can imagine how thrilled I was when I heard about it. I just couldn't believe it. (*To the dog*) Dear, darling Midge …

JACK: How did you hear about it, Mrs Lincoln?

FREDA: I spoke to Leonard this afternoon and he told me about … (*Suddenly*) Incidentally, what's happened to the collar, Mr Kerry – Midge's collar? Was it stolen?

JACK: Yes.

FREDA: Oh dear, it was such a lovely little collar! And it was a present from your father, too, you know – a birthday present.

JACK: (*Watching FREDA*) Curiously enough, the collar was both stolen and returned, Mrs Lincoln.

FREDA: Returned?

JACK: Yes; at the moment Superintendent Bromford's got it.

FREDA: (*Puzzled*) Superintendent Bromford? But why on earth have the police got it? Do they think Midge was stolen then?

The door opens and the taxi driver enters.

WALLY: (*To Freda; annoyed*) Look, I can't stay here all night, lady! I shall be in trouble – real trouble – if you don't get a move on!

FREDA: I'll be with you in a minute.

WALLY: Now please, lady! (*To JACK, nodding towards the street*) There's an officious basket out there – a real stinker!

WALLY returns to his cab. FREDA moves towards the door.

JACK: Mrs Lincoln, before you go – there's something I want to ask you. Did you ever hear my father mention the name Bannister?

FREDA: Bannister? No, I don't think so.

JACK: You've never heard the name before?

FREDA: (*Shaking her head*) No, I haven't. I'm quite good at names, I feel sure I should have remembered it if you father'd mentioned it at all. (*Looking towards the door*) Mr Kerry, you'll have to excuse me …

JACK: Goodbye, Mrs Lincoln, and good luck in the new job.

FREDA: (*Still a shade embarrassed*) Thank you. (*To the poodle*) Say goodbye to Mr Kerry, Midge.

JACK pats the dog, and FREDA goes out onto the street. JACK stands looking at the half-open door. It is difficult to tell what he is thinking.

CUT TO: A Telephone Box in Soho Square, London. Night. *BRENDA THOMPSON is in the telephone box. She has her back to the camera and we do not see her during the telephone conversation. Her handbag is on the ledge by the side of the phone, and she is dialling a number. She stops dialling and after a moment, we hear the number ringing out at the other end.*

CUT TO: The Living Room of JACK KERRY's Flat. Night. *The phone is ringing, and JACK comes out of the kitchen with a sandwich and a glass of milk in his hand. He is wearing a dressing gown over his underclothes. JACK crosses to the telephone and lifts the receiver.*

JACK: (*On the phone*) Juniper 2679.

CUT TO:

BRENDA: (*With a faint north country accent; tensely*) Mr Kerry?

JACK: Yes, speaking …

BRENDA: This is Cathy White, Mr Kerry. I was a friend of Rupert Delaney's …

CUT TO:

JACK: Cathy White!

CUT TO:

BRENDA: I'm in trouble, Mr Kerry, terrible trouble, and I'd like to talk to you before I … give myself up. Can we meet sometime – tonight if possible?

CUT TO:

JACK: (*Tensely*) Yes, of course! Where are you? Where are you speaking from?

CUT TO:

BRENDA: I'm in a restaurant, the Chez Maurice; it's in Greek Street. The top end, near Soho Square.

CUT TO:

JACK: Stay where you are, Miss White! I'll be with you in fifteen minutes!

JACK quickly replaces the phone and runs into the bedroom.

CUT TO: Outside the Chez Maurice Restaurant, Greek Street, Soho. Night.

CATHY WHITE and DOREEN OSBORNE emerge from the restaurant as JACK passes by in a taxi – he is looking out of the window, trying to locate the Chez Maurice. He suddenly sees the two girls and recognises CATHY from the snapshot. DOREEN OSBORNE is nearly thirty, basically a tough woman, but not by any means unattractive. CATHY is younger, prettier, and less experienced. She wears a headscarf which partly helps to conceal her features. JACK's taxi stops in the crowded street about twenty or thirty yards past the restaurant.

DOREEN: Damn, I've left my gloves behind! I'll be with you in a minute, Cathy!

DOREEN goes back into the restaurant and CATHY stands in the doorway, nervously looking up and down Greek Street. She takes a pair of glasses out of her handbag and puts them on. She is obviously on edge, afraid of being recognised. JACK has paid his taxi driver and is waiting for change; he looks across at CATHY who is suddenly aware of the fact that he is taking an interest in her. She turns and looks into the restaurant, anxiously waiting for her friend to return. She steals a glance at JACK who has now received his change and, because of the traffic, has taken temporary refuge on the opposite pavement, watching for an opening in the traffic, so that he can cross the road and join CATHY.

From JACK's point of view CATHY would appear to be waiting for him. He sees her looking at him and gives a nod of recognition. CATHY is puzzled by JACK's nod; puzzled and a shade frightened. She glances into the restaurant again hoping that DOREEN will appear – there is still no sign of her, however, and suddenly, with a quick glance at JACK, CATHY panics and starts running down the street towards Soho Square.

JACK is staggered by CATHY's behaviour and for a brief moment stands on the pavement staring after her, then jumping to the conclusion that she has had second thoughts about their meeting, he gives chase.

DOREEN comes out of the restaurant and is surprised to find that CATHY has vanished. She looks up and down the street.

CATHY is running towards the square; she has lost her glasses and the scarf no longer conceals her hair, let alone her features.

JACK's progress down Greek Street has been unexpectedly impeded by The Mobsters, a pop group who, complete with musical instruments, are pouring out of a dilapidated car onto the pavement. They are searching for one of the lesser- known night spots and the noisiest member of the party takes hold of JACK's arm in an unfortunate attempt to solicit his help.

JACK eventually frees himself but in the process of doing so collides with a middle-aged couple who are also trying to avoid the high-spirited group. JACK apologises, picks up the woman's handbag from the pavement, and pushes his way through a quickly gathering crowd of onlookers attracted by the antics of the long-haired group.

CUT TO: Soho Square. London. Night.
CATHY has reached the square. She stops to regain her breath; undecided which way to go. Suddenly, she sees a cab at the far end of the square – it is about to turn towards Oxford Street,

and CATHY waves frantically for the driver to stop. At first the man doesn't see her, then he spots CATHY out of the corner of his eyes and draws into the kerb.

CUT TO: Outside the Chez Maurice Restaurant, Greek Street, Soho. Night.
A worried looking DOREEN OSBORNE is still standing on the pavement, looking for CATHY.

CUT TO: Soho Square. London. Night.
JACK reaches Soho Square just in time to see CATHY climb into the taxi. He races towards it but before JACK can reach the cab it has gained ground on him and is fast disappearing in the direction of Oxford Street. JACK stands in the square, irritated and annoyed at having lost CATHY. Then a thought occurs to him, and he quickly turns and starts running again, this time in the direction of Charing Cross Road – taking the short cut through Sutton Row.

CUT TO: Inside the Taxi. Night.
CATHY is trying to look out of the back window as the cab turns into Oxford Street and proceeds towards St Giles' Circus. She looks exhausted and a shade frightened – after a moment she turns away from the window and sinks back into the corner. She looks round for her handbag, finds it on the seat, and takes out a cigarette and lighter. Her hand is shaking as she puts the cigarette in her mouth and flicks the lighter. The cab comes to a sudden halt at the traffic lights, and as CATHY lurches forward, she drops the cigarette.

CUT TO:
JACK is now in the Charing Cross Road and racing towards St Giles' Circus.

CUT TO:

JACK reaches the Circus and looks down Oxford Street –
searching for the taxi. He sees several taxis approaching and,
quickly dodging the traffic, crosses to the other side of the road.

CUT TO: Inside the Taxi. Night.

CATHY is leaning back, eyes closed, trying to relax. The cab
slows down as it approaches St Giles' Circus.

CUT TO:

JACK is standing on the kerb, attempting to peer into the
oncoming taxis as they slow down at the lights. Suddenly, he
sees CATHY, and waving to the DRIVER to pull up, he rushes
into the road. As JACK takes hold of the handle RON SMART,
the driver, angrily brakes the cab to a standstill.

RON: What's the game, Mac? Haven't you got any eyes
          in your head? This cab's taken!

JACK: (*With authority*) I'm a police inspector – Detective
          Inspector Kerry. Take us straight to Scotland Yard.

JACK jumps into the cab.

CUT TO: Inside the Taxi. Night.

CATHY, taken by surprise, makes a desperate attempt to leave
the cab by the other door – JACK grabs her by the arm and,
forcing her back into the seat, slams the door closed.

JACK: (*Angrily*) What is this? What the hell are you trying
          to pull?

JACK sits on one of the tip-up seats facing CATHY.

CATHY: (*Tensely*) Who are you? What do you want?

JACK: You know damn well who I am! I'm Jack Kerry –
          Inspector Kerry. You phoned me …

CATHY: I – I did?

JACK: Why, yes!

CATHY: (*Shaking her head*) No …

JACK: You said you wanted to see me, you said …

JACK stops. CATHY is staring at him, slowly shaking her head.

JACK: You mean – it wasn't you on the phone?

CATHY: No … No, it wasn't.

JACK looks at CATHY; he begins to realise what has happened.

CATHY: Did someone really phone you, pretending to be me?

JACK: Yes.

CATHY: (*Tensely*) It was a tip-off … They knew I was at the restaurant.

JACK: Who's "they"?

There is a pause; CATHY doesn't answer.

JACK: We've been looking all over for you, we want to question you about the Delaney murder.

CATHY: I didn't kill Rupert. I didn't have anything to do with it.

JACK: We're not suggesting you did, but we've still got to question you.

CATHY: I don't know anything about the murder. There's nothing I can tell you.

JACK: There's a great deal you can tell us! You've been living with Delaney. You've been living with him for over a month now.

CATHY is tense but a little more sure of herself now.

CATHY: I'm sorry, I can't help you.

JACK looks at CATHY, leans forward, and is a shade more friendly.

JACK: Cathy, listen – if you didn't kill Delaney then believe me, the best thing you can do …

CATHY: (*Angrily, almost vehement*) Don't call me Cathy! When I want you to call me Cathy, I'll say so!

There is a pause.

CATHY: (*Softly*) Where are you taking me?

59

JACK: To Scotland Yard – I want you to meet a friend of
          mine. Inspector Royce. He's in charge of the case.

CATHY: (*Nodding*) I know Royce.

JACK: You know him?

CATHY: I've seen him around. Ed Royce. I'm glad he's a
          friend of <u>yours</u>.

*JACK is surprised by CATHY's remark, but he makes no
comment – then, glancing down, he sees the cigarette on the
floor. He takes out his cigarette case and offers her one. She
hesitates then takes a cigarette. JACK feels in his pocket for his
lighter but by the time he has found it CATHY is using her own.
JACK slowly puts his lighter away. CATHY sits smoking the
cigarette, looking at JACK. She is still tense, and on edge, but
far more sure of herself. JACK is aware of this.*

CATHY: Do we have to go to Scotland Yard?

JACK: Yes, I'm afraid we do.

CATHY: Couldn't we go somewhere else?

After a moment.

JACK: Where – for instance?

After a moment.

CATHY: Your flat.

JACK: (*Looking at CATHY*) Why should I take you to my
          flat – Miss White? Give me one good reason, Miss
          White?

CATHY: We could talk better.

JACK: I thought you didn't want to talk?

CATHY: I don't – not about Rupert. But if we go to your flat,
          we could talk about other things.

JACK: What kind of things?

A pause.

JACK: What kind of things, Miss White?

CATHY: We – we could talk about your father, for instance
          …

JACK leans forward.

JACK: (*Tensely*) What do you know about my father?
CATHY hesitates, then:
CATHY: I know who killed him.

END OF EPISODE TWO

,

EPISODE THREE

OPEN TO: The Living room of JACK KERRY's Flat. Night.

CATHY WHITE is sitting on the settee watching JACK who is mixing her a drink. Although CATHY still looks tense and worried, she is obviously a little more sure of herself than she was in the taxi. She takes a lipstick out of her handbag and is nervously using it when JACK turns and brings the drink over to her.

CATHY: Aren't you going to have one?

JACK: Not at the moment.

CATHY replaces the lipstick in her handbag and taking the drink, putting the bag down on the edge of the settee – it falls to the floor. JACK casually picks it up and, a shade surprised by its weight, glances at the handbag as he puts it down again on the settee. JACK sits on the arm of the settee, looking down at CATHY.

CATHY: That girl – the one that phoned you – the one that said she was me ...

JACK: Yes?

CATHY: You don't happen to remember whether she had an accent?

JACK: Yes, she had – a slight North Country accent.

CATHY: Did she sound as if ...

JACK: (*Interrupting CATHY*) Miss White, I didn't bring you here to talk about that phone call, I brought you here because in the taxi you said you knew who killed my father.

CATHY: (*Softly*) Yes ... (*She looks at Jack; hesitates, then suddenly:*) If I tell you about your father, if I tell you what happened the night before he was killed, will you promise me that ...

JACK: Look, let's get one thing straight! I'm not in a position to promise you anything!

CATHY: (*Softly*) What do you mean?

JACK: I'm not investigating the Delaney murder. Right
           now, in fact, I'm not officially investigating
           anything. I'm on leave. (*He rises, agitated*) I took
           a risk in bringing you here instead of taking you to
           the Yard – one hell of a risk – but if you'll tell me
           all you know about my father then I'll try and help
           you. (*Shaking his head*) I can't say any more than
           that.

CATHY looks at the glass she is holding, hesitates, then drinks.
JACK sits down again on the arm of the settee.

CATHY: (*After a moment*) I met Rupert about a year ago. I'm
           an actress, well – a dancer really – and Rupert saw
           me in a show in Liverpool. He tried to persuade me
           to come down to London, but I wasn't very keen on
           the idea then. I was doing pretty well up north and
           I just didn't see any point in sticking my neck out
           down here. A few months ago, I changed my mind
           and … I went into a revue at the Saint Edward's. It
           was a flop.

JACK: Yes, I know.

CATHY: (*Nodding*) While the show was on, I was in digs in
           Notting Hill Gate but when it closed, I moved in
           with Rupert. He'd been wanting me to do this for
           some time but I'd always … Anyway, it worked out
           better than I thought it would. We were very happy
           together – at first, at any rate …

JACK: Go on …

CATHY: He always seemed to have plenty of money, and I
           must admit he was pretty generous with it. He told
           me that he was in the property business and that an
           uncle of his had died just after the war and had left
           him a quarter of a million. One night last week – it
           was the night before your father was killed – we
           went to a cocktail party. We were both feeling

pretty high when we arrived back at the flat. It was about half past ten …

CUT TO: The Drawing Room of RUPERT DELANEY's Flat, Knightsbridge, London. Night.

This is a large, pleasant room, furnished in contemporary style. The whole flat has been placed in the hands of an interior decorator at some time or other, although it still manages to reflect a little of DELANEY's personality.

RUPERT and CATHY enter from the hall. It is quite obvious that they have been to a party. RUPERT switches on the record player, then returns to CATHY and stands smiling at her for a moment; suddenly, he takes hold of her and pulls her down onto the settee.

CATHY: (*Laughing*) Hi, what is this?

RUPERT: My God, what a dull party!

CATHY: It wasn't that dull!

RUPERT: That corny old story about the psychiatrist … And who on earth was that little woman with the large behind?

CATHY: I don't know, I've never seen her before. She couldn't speak a word of English.

RUPERT: (*Kissing CATHY*) She got by!

CATHY: (*Laughing*) Darling, what time's your plane tomorrow?

RUPERT: Twelve o'clock. We'll be in Paris for lunch. (*Looking at CATHY*) You know, I just don't believe what you say! You've been to Paris before, you must have been!

CATHY: No, darling, I haven't. Honestly, I haven't.

RUPERT: You mean, you've never been to the Tour d'Argent – the Lido – Maxims?

CATHY shakes her head and pulls a sad face.

CATHY: No …

67

RUPERT: My God, sweetie, you really are a peasant!
RUPERT and CATHY laugh, and as RUPERT draws CATHY
towards him the door bell rings.
RUPERT: Oh, hell!
CATHY: (*Surprised*) Are you expecting anyone?
RUPERT: No.
CATHY: Well, who is it?
RUPERT: (*A shade irritated*) I don't know, Cathy.
CATHY: (*Rising*) I'll go.
RUPERT: (*Stopping her*) No. No, I'll take it.
RUPERT gets up from the settee, and crosses into the hall.
CATHY stands watching him. RUPERT enters the hall and
opens the front door. CHARLES BANNISTER is standing in the
doorway; he wears a little overcoat over a dinner jacket and
looks faintly agitated.
BANNISTER: Thank goodness you're in! I've been trying to
              phone you. What the devil's the matter with
              that phone of yours?
RUPERT: Come in, Charles. (*As BANNISTER enters the*
              hall) I've been out all evening.
BANNISTER: I won't come in, I just want a quick word with
              you.
BANNISTER stands in the hall, hesitating. RUPERT looks at
him, he is curious.
RUPERT: What is it, Charles? Has something happened?
BANNISTER: Yes, Mel Harris phoned me. He's been talking
              to Mrs Lincoln, and he's found that Kerry's
              going to be at the golf … (*He hesitates, then:*)
              I'm afraid it's tomorrow morning, Rupert.
RUPERT: (*Shocked*) What do you mean?
BANNISTER: You know damn well what I mean! Bob Kerry
              … Tomorrow morning, ten o'clock, Highgate
              Golf Club.

RUPERT: Charles, it's no use, I can't do it! I've thought about this; I've thought about nothing else ever since ...

BANNISTER: Look, Rupert, we've been through all this – we've been through it a thousand times! (*Patting RUPERT's arm*) Now you be there tomorrow morning; ten o'clock, sharp, there's a good fellow.

CATHY appears from the drawing room. She has heard the conversation and is faintly puzzled by it.

BANNISTER: (*Surprised*) Hello, Cathy! (*Glancing at RUPERT*) I didn't know you were here.

CATHY: Aren't you coming in for a drink, Charles?

BANNISTER: No – no, thank you. I was passing and I just wanted a quick word with Rupert about something, that's all. (*To RUPERT*) Not to worry, old man. Everything'll be all right. Mel knows what he's doing. (*He turns, smiling at CATHY*) That's a lovely dress, Cathy.

CATHY: Thank you – I'm glad you like it. How's Iris these days?

BANNISTER: Oh, she's fine.

CATHY: I haven't seen her for ages.

BANNISTER: She's been pretty busy, you know how it is. And we've been going down to Aldeburgh most weekends. We're looking for a cottage down there.

CATHY: Won't you really join us for a drink, Charles?

BANNISTER: No, no, I won't, Cathy, thank you. I must be off. Good night, my dear.

CATHY: Good night.

CHARLES looks at RUPERT, nods to him, then goes out, closing the front door behind him. RUPERT doesn't move: he looks tense and drawn.

CATHY: What is it, Rupert?

RUPERT ignores her and walks back into the drawing room. He crosses to the record player and switches it off; standing with his back to CATHY who has followed him from the hall.

CATHY: What is it? What's happened?

RUPERT: I'm afraid the Paris trip is off – for the time being, at any rate.

CATHY moves over to RUPERT.

CATHY: (*Disappointed*) Oh, no …

RUPERT: I'm sorry, Cathy.

CATHY: But why is it off? What's happening tomorrow?

RUPERT: I'm playing golf. I fixed it up ages ago and forgot all about it.

RUPERT crosses to the drinks table and starts to mix himself a drink.

CATHY: Golf? But surely to God you can cancel a game of golf!

RUPERT: (*Tensely; turning*) Look, Cathy – I'm sorry, but there's nothing I can do about this. Just nothing.

CATHY again moves across to RUPERT.

CATHY: It's Harris, isn't it?

RUPERT: What do you mean?

CATHY: It's always the same, isn't it, Rupert? Mel Harris says "Jump," so you jump!

RUPERT turns on CATHY viciously.

RUPERT: Shut up!

CATHY looks at RUPERT, she is desperately near to tears, then turns away.

RUPERT: This hasn't got anything to do with Mel Harris. And I've told you before, don't mention his name – ever. To me or anyone else – you understand?

CATHY: (*Quietly, hurt*) Yes, Rupert, I understand.

RUPERT glares at CATHY, angry and overwrought. Suddenly, he turns and throws the glass he is holding across the room.

RUPERT: Hell – hell – hell …

CUT TO: The Living Room of JACK KERRY's Flat. Night.
JACK is still sitting on the arm of the settee listening to CATHY.

CATHY: The next morning he still looked worried and, if anything, even more overwrought than the night before. I tried to get him to change his mind, about Paris, I mean – but he wouldn't. He left the flat about half past eight and said he'd be back some time during the afternoon.

JACK: Go on …

CATHY: Later that morning – I think it was about half past eleven – he phoned me and said that there'd been an accident and he was on his way home. He didn't say what the accident was, and I jumped to the conclusion it was something to do with his car. Rupert was a careless driver and he'd been involved in one or two incidents. I was in the kitchen when he arrived.

CUT TO: The Drawing Room of RUPERT DELANEY's Flat, Knightsbridge, London. Morning.
CATHY comes running out of the kitchen as RUPERT enters from the hall. He wears a blazer, dark grey trousers, and carries a raincoat over his arm. He is still tense, but is trying to control himself, realising that he has a difficult situation ahead of him.

CATHY: Rupert, are you all right?

RUPERT: Yes. (*Quickly*) Has anyone called?

CATHY: No.

RUPERT: No one?

CATHY: No, no one. Darling, what happened?

RUPERT: Did anyone phone or …

CATHY: (*Shaking her head*) No, there's hasn't been anything, not since you left. Rupert, what is it? What's all this about an accident?

RUPERT: (*Not looking at CATHY; hesitantly*) I – I killed a man this morning ...

CATHY: (*Shocked*) What!

RUPERT: ... Accidentally, of course, on the golf course. He was in a bunker and unfortunately my ball hit him and ... he fell down and struck his head on something ...

CATHY: Oh, Rupert!

RUPERT: (*Still not looking at CATHY*) I was on my own, practising ... I – I didn't see him. I was standing on the tee and ... (*Defiantly, almost trying to convince himself it happened*) It was just bloody bad luck – there was nothing I could do about it! Nothing!

CATHY: Yes, of course, but – (*Puzzled*) what were you doing on your own? I thought you'd arranged to play with ...

RUPERT: The others didn't turn up; I waited for about an hour and then decided to ... play a few holes on my own.

CATHY looks at RUPERT; she realises that he is not telling her the truth. RUPERT crosses to the drinks table; he stands looking down at the bottles.

CATHY: (*Quietly*) Did you know the man?

RUPERT turns, pretending not to have heard.

RUPERT: What?

CATHY: The man that was killed – did you know him?

RUPERT: No, I'd never seen him before.

RUPERT lifts one of the bottles from the table and looks at it.

CATHY: Who was he?

RUPERT: His name was Kerry.

CATHY: (*Surprised*) Kerry?

CATHY moves across to RUPERT.

72

RUPERT: (*Turning*) Yes.

CATHY: But that was the name Charles mentioned, last night.

RUPERT: (*Looking at CATHY; softly*) No, you're mistaken.

CATHY: I'm not mistaken, Rupert!

RUPERT: I tell you you're mistaken!

CATHY: (*Adamantly*) Darling, I was listening! I heard it quite distinctly. I heard Charles say: "Bob Kerry. Highgate Golf Club." Then you said …

RUPERT suddenly drops the bottle he is holding onto the table and grabs CATHY by the arms.

RUPERT: (*Tensely*) Cathy … Cathy, listen to me!

CATHY: Rupert, you're hurting my arm!

RUPERT: You've got to listen to me!

CATHY: Rupert, my arm!

RUPERT: (*Releasing CATHY*) I'm sorry – I'm sorry, sweetie.

After a moment, RUPERT takes hold of CATHY again, gently.

RUPERT: I'm in trouble, real trouble, Cathy. You've got to help me.

CATHY: What is it? What is it you want me to do?

RUPERT: I – I want you to forget about last night.

CATHY: Last night? You mean about Charles and …

RUPERT: Yes. I don't want you to repeat what you heard. I want you to forget that Charles came here last night. No matter what happens – no matter what you read in the newspapers – I want you to forget about last night. Completely, Cathy.

CATHY: (*After a moment*) All right, Rupert – if that's what you want.

RUPERT: That's what I want, sweetie. Is it a promise?

CATHY: (*Worried and puzzled*) Yes …

RUPERT: Are you sure?

CATHY nods.

RUPERT: No more questions?

CATHY slowly shakes her head. RUPERT takes her in his arms and kisses her, finally holding her close to him. We hear CATHY's voice as the camera slowly tracks in on her face staring into space over RUPERT's shoulder.

CATHY's VOICE: When I read about the accident, I was very worried. I knew that Rupert hadn't told me the truth and I had a feeling – a horrible feeling – that your father's death wasn't accidental. I kept remembering the conversation I'd heard the night before between Rupert and Charles Bannister …

CUT TO: The Living Room of JACK KERRY's Flat. Night. *JACK is listening to CATHY as she continues with her story.*

CATHY: Then early one morning – the morning of the Inquest – Rupert received a phone call from Mel Harris. I was only half awake at the time, and he took the call in the living room, but I'm sure I heard him say … (*She hesitates*)

JACK: Go on …

CATHY: I'm sure I heard Rupert say, "Mel, remember this – you killed Kerry, I didn't. Now for God's sake leave me alone!" When he came back into the bedroom, he was furious, almost trembling with rage. I – I was so frightened I pretended to be asleep.

JACK rises and taking the glass from CATHY puts it down on the table.

JACK: (*Quietly, yet with authority*) This man Harris – Mel Harris. (*Moving towards CATHY*) Tell me all you know about him.

CATHY: (*Shaking her head*) I don't know anything about him. Except that he used to phone Rupert every morning and they'd talk for half an hour, even an hour some days. But he never came to the flat and, so far as I know, I've never seen him.

JACK: What did they talk about?

CATHY: Business. I told you, Rupert has something to do with property. So had Mel Harris. Judging from their phone conversations they used to buy and sell property all over the place.

JACK: Were they in business together?

CATHY: Yes – Harris was the boss.

JACK: What makes you say that?

CATHY: It was obvious. If Mel Harris said "Go to Birmingham, or Leeds, or Manchester" Rupert went. There was never any argument about it.

JACK: (*Nodding*) And Charles Bannister – how does he fit into the picture?

CATHY: Charles was a friend of Rupert's. He and his wife used to come to the flat quite often. It was through Charles that Rupert met Mel Harris.

JACK: I see. (*He looks at CATHY*) Is Bannister in the property business too?

CATHY: No, I don't think so. He's a retired stockbroker.

JACK: (*Suddenly*) Okay, Miss White – now tell me …

CATHY: Cathy, please! I'm sorry I was rude to you in the taxi.

JACK looks at CATHY for a moment.

JACK: Tell me about last night.

CATHY: Rupert took me out to dinner and we … (*She hesitates*)

JACK: You had a row?

CATHY: Yes, a terrible row. That's why I left him.

JACK: What time was this?

CATHY: About ten o'clock.

JACK: Where did you leave him, in the restaurant?

CATHY: No, we left the restaurant together at about half past nine and drove into the park. We sat in his car for about half an hour.

JACK: And then what happened?

CATHY: I – I told you, I left him.

JACK: And what did you do?

CATHY: I went for a walk.

JACK: Alone?

CATHY: Yes, of course.

JACK: Where did you walk?

CATHY: In the park most of the time.

JACK: Did you talk to anyone – see anyone you knew?

CATHY: (*Looking at JACK*) No … No, I'm afraid I didn't …

JACK: Go on – then what happened?

CATHY: I – I stayed the night with a friend of mine. (*Distressed*) I wish to God I hadn't now, I wish I'd gone back to the flat. Perhaps if I'd done that … (*Shaking her head*) If only we hadn't had that bloody silly little row …

JACK: (*After a moment*) What was the row about, Cathy?

CATHY: (*Still distressed*) Oh, it was nothing.

JACK: Was it about my father – about what happened?

CATHY: No, it was about the silliest thing …

The front door bell rings.

JACK: What was it, Cathy?

CATHY: It really wasn't about anything important.

JACK: Well – what was it about?

CATHY: It was just that …

CATHY stops speaking and looks towards the hall. The front door bell is still ringing. JACK also turns towards the hall, then looks at CATHY again.

JACK: Go on …

CATHY: We had a row about – a dog collar. (*Distressed, yet unable to control a nervous little laugh*) I told you, didn't I? I told you it wasn't important.

JACK stares at CATHY, hesitates, then goes out into the hall.

CUT TO: Outside the Front Door of JACK KERRY's Flat. Night.

CLEG REED is standing, gun in hand, flat against the wall. He is waiting for JACK to open the front door. CLEG is a tough, unpleasant, dandified looking man in his late twenties.

CUT TO: The Hall of JACK KERRY's Flat. Night.

JACK reaches the front door and opens it. There is no one there. He is obviously surprised and is about to start out into the corridor when he sees the envelope. CLEG REED has placed a large envelope, too big for the letter box, on the mat outside the front door. Without thinking, JACK bends down to pick up the envelope and almost immediately realises the mistake he is making. As he half turns, a vicious blow, from CLEGG's gun, catches him on the back of his head and he falls forward, collapsing unconscious onto the mat.

CUT TO: Outside the Front Door of JACK KERRY's Flat. Night.

The front door is half open and JACK is still lying on the mat, slowly regaining consciousness. The envelope has vanished. JACK sits up and looks about him. Suddenly, he remembers CATHY and, realising what has happened, jumps to his feet. The pain in his head is far worse than he expected, and he leans against the wall, holding his head in his hands. Gradually, he begins to feel a little better and after a moment he goes into the flat, leaving the front door open.

CUT TO: The Living Room of JACK KERRY's Flat. Night.

JACK enters the room calling, "Cathy". He sees immediately that the room is empty and dashing across to the bedroom throws open the door, shouting for CATHY again as he does so. The bedroom is empty.

JACK quickly looks into the kitchen and the other rooms, calling CATHY's name as he opens the doors. There is no sign of CATHY in the flat. Worried, and still obviously in pain from the blow on his head, JACK crosses down to the settee. He is holding on to the arm of the settee when he hears ED's voice calling from the hall.

ED's VOICE: Can I come in?

JACK slowly turns and sees ED ROYCE standing in the hall. An attaché case is in his hand.

ED: The door was open, so I thought ... (*Moving across to JACK*) What is it, Jack? (*Faintly alarmed*) What's the matter?

JACK: I – I went to answer the door. There was a letter on the mat and when I stopped to pick it up some bastard hit me with ... with ...

JACK suddenly sways and is about to fall forward when ED catches him.

JACK: (*Holding on to ED*) I'll be all right, Ed. I'm just a bit dizzy, that's all.

ED looks at JACK.

JACK: I'll be all right in a minute ...

CUT TO: The Living Room of JACK KERRY's Flat. Night. *ED ROYCE is standing by the table, smoking a cigarette and talking to JACK, who is now sitting on the settee. Both men look faintly annoyed with each other, and as JACK talks ED turns and stubs out his cigarette in an ashtray. JACK has a drink in his hand. It is obvious that he has now fully recovered from the blow on his head.*

JACK: ... It's very easy to criticise, Ed – dead easy – but what would you have done under the circumstances?

ED: You know damn well what I would have done! I'd have taken her back to the Yard.

JACK:	(*Quietly*) I wonder …
ED:	Jack, you were an idiot to bring that girl back here, and an even bigger idiot to let her slip through your fingers like that! (*Agitated*) What the hell are we going to tell Bromford?
JACK:	(*Irritated*) I'm not interested in Bromford!
ED:	Well, I am and I'm investigating this case. You might try and remember that. (*Crosses to the settee*) When the Superintendent hears about this he'll go up like a flaming rocket!
JACK:	Does he have to hear about it?
ED:	(*Looking at JACK*) What do you mean?
JACK:	If I can find Cathy again, if I can find her before …
ED:	(*Interrupting JACK*) If – if – if! Your only chance is another tip-off, and you know it! You wouldn't have picked her up tonight if it hadn't been for that phone call. She knew she was wanted by the police – she knew we were looking for her – so why the hell didn't she give herself up?
JACK:	You know perfectly well why she didn't give herself up! She was frightened.
ED:	Frightened of what? If she didn't kill Delaney, what has she to be frightened of?
JACK:	Ed, for Pete's sake! This girl was living with Delaney, she had a row with him, and her alibi wasn't worth a cup of cold tea! Can you blame her for not going to the police?
ED:	Yes, well – I still say you shouldn't have brought her here.
JACK:	(*Rising from the settee*) All right, so I made a mistake! It isn't the first one I've made, and I don't suppose it'll be the last.

ED: (*After a moment, a decision:*) Jack, I'll tell you
           what I'll do. I'll keep my mouth shut about tonight
           …

JACK: Thank you, Ed …

ED: … I'll say nothing for forty-eight hours. (*He moves
           to JACK*) But if you haven't found Cathy White by
           this time on Thursday, I'll tell Bromford exactly
           what happened tonight, I'll tell him the whole story.
           I shall have to, Jack.

JACK: (*Quietly, after a little nod:*) Okay. Now you tell me
           something, and be honest about it.

ED: Go on …

JACK: Do you believe her story? Do you believe what she
           told me?

ED: I believe part of it. I think she was telling the truth
           about your father, about what happened the night
           before he was killed. But I don't think she was
           telling the truth about Delaney.

JACK: Why do you say that?

ED: Because I don't believe Delaney was in the
           property racket. I think he was playing a very
           different game.

JACK: What do you mean?

ED: I think Cathy White told the truth when she said he
           was working for that man – what was his name?

JACK: Mel Harris.

ED: But it's my bet Harris runs a call-girl set-up, and
           runs it on a very big scale.

JACK: And you think Cathy knew this?

ED: Of course, she knew it! The property story was just
           a cover-up, for your benefit.

JACK: (*Shaking his head*) I don't agree. I'm sorry, Ed, I
           don't agree.

ED smiles and crosses to his attaché case, which is by the side of the settee.

ED: (*Picking up the case*) No, I didn't think you would. (*With heavy sarcasm*) Have you read any good books lately?

JACK: (*Not really friendly*) Oh, I know what you're thinking! I know what's at the back of that sordid little mind of yours. But you're mistaken.

ED: That makes two of us.

ED opens the attaché case and takes out the dog collar.

ED: Here's the collar. We've finished with it.

JACK: Have the labs seen it?

ED: They've all seen it – it's been right through the building. The report's negative. It's just a perfectly ordinary dog collar. What the devil Delaney meant by the note of his I can't imagine.

JACK: No, neither can I.

JACK takes the collar from ED and looks at it.

ED: (*After a moment*) What was it he said – "This is why your father was killed"?

JACK: (*Quietly; still looking at the collar*) Yes …

CUT TO: The Front of JACK KERRY's Flat. Night.

A tall, well-dressed man wearing a bowler hat and carrying an umbrella is standing in front of the door. His finger is on the button, and we hear the bell ringing inside the flat. Since there appears to be no reply, LEONARD LINCOLN moves away and consults his pocket watch; at this moment the door opens. We see JACK, wearing dressing-gown and pyjamas standing in the hall.

LEONARD: Oh – er – Mr Kerry?

JACK: (*Surprised*) Yes?

LEONARD: I – I do hope I haven't disturbed you, Mr Kerry. I'm sorry, dropping in on you unannounced like this.

JACK: Who are you? What do you want?

LEONARD: Oh, I beg your pardon. I'm Mrs Lincoln's nephew – Leonard Lincoln. We haven't actually met before but I'm sure we've heard a great deal about each other from my aunt.

JACK: Yes, of course! I'm sorry, Mr Lincoln … Do come in, please …

LEONARD: Thank you. (*As he enters*) It's very remiss of me, dropping in like this – I do apologise.

CUT TO: The Living room of JACK KERRY's Flat. Night.
JACK enters followed by LEONARD LINCOLN.

JACK: Can I get you a drink?

LEONARD: That's most kind of you, but – I'm afraid I don't drink.

JACK: (*Indicating a box on the table*) Cigarette?

LEONARD: I'm afraid I don't smoke either. No vices, Mr Kerry – except one, perhaps. (*Smiling*) I have a disturbing habit of coming straight to the point, at least so my colleagues tell me.

JACK: I wouldn't have said that was necessarily a vice, Mr Lincoln – in my job we'd consider it a virtue.

LEONARD: (*With a little laugh*) Yes – yes, I suppose you would. (*A moment, then:*) Mr Kerry, I'm worried about my aunt, quite disturbed about her in fact, and I thought I'd very much like to have a word with you about it.

JACK: What are you disturbed about? Incidentally, you know of course that your aunt isn't with me any longer?

LEONARD: Yes; yes, I know. I understand she's working at that new hotel in Knightsbridge, The Royal – or something-or-other. Royal Plaza, I think it is.

JACK: Yes, that's right. Do sit down, Mr Lincoln.

LEONARD: Thank you. (*He looks around the room, finally deciding on the settee*) I'm very fond of my aunt and I owe her a great deal. You see, both my parents died when I was fourteen and my aunt immediately … Anyway, that's a long and rather tedious story. The point is, I'm worried about her, Mr Kerry. I think she's well, not to put too fine a point on it – I think she's going round the bend.

JACK: Why do you say that?

LEONARD: Well – it's most extraordinary; she's telephoned me three times since she's been in this new job and she always talks about the same thing.

JACK: What's that?

LEONARD: She always talks about you, Mr Kerry. She says – this is quite absurd, and I do apologise for mentioning it – she says you stole something from her.

JACK: Stole something?

LEONARD: Yes.

JACK: What am I supposed to have stolen, Mr Lincoln?

LEONARD: That's just it, it's quite ridiculous. She says you've stolen a dog collar.

JACK looks at LEONARD for a moment.

JACK: I presume she means the collar my father gave her?

LEONARD: Yes, that's right. She keeps on about that, how devoted she was to your father. But I really fail to see what on earth that's got to do with it. I knew she was distressed, very distressed – but now that she's got the dog back surely to goodness she can forget about the collar. In any case, she can well afford to buy the wretched animal another one. I've even offered to buy it one myself.

JACK crosses to the desk.

JACK: Yes, but it isn't another collar she wants, Mr Lincoln.

JACK opens a drawer in the desk and takes out the collar.

JACK: It's this one.

LEONARD rises, obviously surprised and goes across to JACK.

LEONARD: Is this the collar she's making all the fuss about?

JACK: Yes.

LEONARD: Good Lod! (*Holding out his hand*) May I?

JACK: Yes, of course.

LEONARD takes the collar and examines it. JACK watches him.

LEONARD: (*Returning the collar to JACK*) It's a very nice one, very nice, but I fail to see what all the excitement's about.

JACK: So do I, Lincoln. (*He puts the collar down on the desk*) Anyway, you can tell your aunt if she gets in touch with me, she can have it back.

LEONARD: Really? Oh, well – that solves the problem. Thank you, Mr Kerry, I'm very grateful to you.

LEONARD returns to the settee, and, picking up his hat and umbrella, crosses towards the hall. As the two enter the hall and move towards the front door, LEONARD hesitates.

LEONARD: It's none of my business – and I hope you don't mind my asking – but why didn't you give my aunt the collar the other day, when she picked up the poodle?

JACK: I didn't give it to her for the simple reason that I hadn't got it. Superintendent Bromford had it.

LEONARD: But what on earth was the Superintendent doing with it?

JACK: (*Noncommittally*) He was taking a look at it, Mr Lincoln. But you know, I told your aunt this. I told her the collar was at Scotland Yard.

LEONARD: Really? Well, there you are, you see! She never told me that! Never said a blessed word about it! (*Shaking hands*) Thank you, Mr Kerry.

JACK opens the front door.

JACK: Ask Mrs Lincoln to give me a ring.

LEONARD: Yes, I'll certainly do that – and again, many thanks. Good night.

JACK: Good night.

As LEONARD goes out, JACK closes the door. He returns to the living room and is thoughtfully going towards the bedroom when he sees the dog collar on the desk. He crosses to the desk, picks up the collar and hesitates. Then opening the desk takes out a bunch of keys.

CUT TO: The Office of Bob Kerry Ltd. Night.

JACK comes down the spiral staircase carrying the bunch of keys and the dog collar. He switches on the office light and then crosses to the safe. He opens the safe, puts the collar inside, and turns back towards the staircase. As he passes DOUGLAS's desk, he notices that a file has slipped to the floor – various letters and documents are on the carpet, some wedged between the chair and the desk. He picks up the papers,

puts them on the desk, and begins to sort them out – as he does so, his eye falls on a book which lies open in front of him.
It is a copy of the A.A. Members Handbook. Something in the book arouses JACK's interest and he picks it up and looks at it. The book is open at details relating to Aldeburgh, Suffolk. JACK continues to look at the book for a moment, then thoughtfully returns it to the desk, carefully placing it in the same position as before. He looks across at the telephone, then picks up the receiver.

CUT TO: A Telephone on a small bedside table.
The phone rings and SUPERINTENDENT BROMFORD appears. He is wearing pyjamas and holds a toothbrush in his hand.
BROMFORD: (*Irritated*) Putney 7824 …
JACK's VOICE: Superintendent Bromford?
BROMFORD: Speaking …

CUT TO:
JACK: I'm sorry to bother you at this time of night, sir – this is Jack Kerry.

CUT TO:
BROMFORD: What can I do for you, Kerry?

CUT TO:
JACK: If I remember rightly, sir, when you saw the Bannisters, they were just off somewhere … Can you, by any chance, remember where they were going, sir?

CUT TO:
BROMFORD: Yes – they were going down to Aldeburgh.

86

CUT TO:

JACK: Aldeburgh, in Suffolk?

CUT TO:

BROMFORD: Yes, I think it's in Suffolk. Why? What's this all about, Kerry?

CUT TO:

JACK: (*Quickly*) Thank you. That's all I wanted to know. Goodnight, sir, sorry to have troubled you.

JACK replaces the telephone. He looks down at the open A.A. book on the desk.

CUT TO: The Office of Bob Kerry Ltd. Morning.

DOUGLAS is standing by the desk looking through a file of letters. LIZ MASON can be seen in the shop, talking to a customer. DOUGLAS is reading a letter when JACK comes down the staircase. He turns.

DOUGLAS: Good morning.

JACK: Good morning, Douglas.

DOUGLAS: We've had a letter from a firm in Inverness called Fairways Limited, they say they used to do business with us about five years ago. Do you remember them?

JACK: (*Crossing to the desk*) What do they make?

DOUGLAS: Well, they used to make sweaters but apparently, they've switched over to swimsuits. (*He looks at the letter*) Tartan bikinis a speciality.

JACK laughs, and then casually points to the A.A. book on the desk.

JACK: Is this yours, Doug?

DOUGLAS: No, I borrowed it from Liz.

DOUGLAS picks up the book and puts it in the drawer.

DOUGLAS: I wanted to look up something.

JACK nods and moves across to the safe, takes the keys out of his pocket. The telephone rings and DOUGLAS answers it.

DOUGLAS: (*On the phone*) Bob Kerry Limited … Who is that? … (*Surprised*) Yes, he is, hold on a minute. (*To JACK*) It's for you – it's Mrs Lincoln.

JACK looks at DOUGLAS, then puts the keys back in his pocket, crosses to the desk and takes the telephone. DOUGLAS goes out of the office and joins LIZ in the shop.

JACK: (*On the phone*) … Good morning, Mrs Lincoln.

CUT TO: A Telephone Box. Knightsbridge. London. Morning.

FREDA LINCOLN is on the telephone. She looks nervous and a shade embarrassed.

FREDA: Hello, Mr Kerry … I'm sorry to bother you but I've just been talking to Leonard, my nephew. He tells me he saw you last night?

CUT TO:

JACK: He did, Mrs Lincoln. We had quite an interesting little chat.

CUT TO:

FREDA: I – I understand you've got the collar back – Midge's collar?

CUT TO:

JACK: Yes, I have. (*Pleasantly*) Would you like it?

CUT TO:

FREDA: (*Speaking quickly, obviously relieved by the suggestion:*) Yes, I would, Mr Kerry! Thank you very much. Would you be kind enough to post it to me? My address is …

CUT TO:

JACK: (*Interrupting FREDA*) No, I'm sorry, Mrs Lincoln, but I'd rather not post it. As a matter of fact, I want something from you, too. Call it a swap if you like.

CUT TO:

FREDA: What – what is it you want?

CUT TO:

JACK: Information.

CUT TO:

FREDA: Information – about what?

CUT TO:

JACK: About a friend of yours – Mel Harris.

CUT TO:

FREDA: I – I don't know anyone called Mel Harris.

CUT TO:

JACK: I think you do, Mrs Lincoln. (*He is apparently about to ring off*) The collar's here if you want it, drop in the flat any time.

CUT TO:

FREDA: No, wait a minute! I – I don't want to come to the flat – it's not convenient. I … (*Suddenly*) Do you know a pub – The Golden Plough?

CUT TO:

JACK: In St John's Wood?

CUT TO:

FREDA: Yes. Meet me there this evening, Mr Kerry, about seven o'clock. I'll be in the saloon bar …

FREDA rings off.

CUT TO:

JACK thoughtfully replaces his receiver.

CUT TO: The Saloon Bar of The Golden Plough, St John's Wood. London. Night.

This is a modern style bar with a horseshoe shaped bar and various small tables. On the right of the bar there is a door with the "Ladies Room" symbol on it.

Several of the tables are already occupied and a white-coated waiter – CECIL – is busy behind the bar. NORMAN PENN is standing in the centre of the room fondling a Siamese cat he is holding; he is wearing his hat and coat, and is obviously waiting for someone. There is a background of soft music.

JACK enters from the street. PENN immediately recognises him. On hearing the name "Kerry" mentioned, CECIL looks across at JACK.

PENN: (*Surprised*) Why, hello, Mr Kerry! Good evening …

JACK: Oh, hello, Mr Penn!

They both shake hands.

JACK: How are you?

PENN: I'm very well, thank you, sir. I haven't seen you here before. Is this one of your usual haunts?

JACK: No, I'm afraid it isn't; I'm meeting a friend of mine. I suppose this is your local?

PENN: Yes, my shop's only just round the corner.

DOREEN OSBORNE comes out of the Ladies Room and stops dead as she sees JACK talking to NORMAN PENN. For a brief moment, she is undecided what to do, then quickly making up her mind to brazen out the situation, she crosses to the two men.

DOREEN: (*To PENN*) I'm ready, duckie!

DOREEN takes the cat from PENN.

DOREEN: Has Chou been behaving himself?

PENN: Yes – he's been as good as gold.

DOREEN: (*To the cat*) No tiddles, eh? Good boy!

DOREEN smiles at JACK, who is now looking at her, and moves towards the door.

JACK: Excuse me … Aren't you a friend of Cathy White's?

PENN looks at JACK, then at DOREEN. He says nothing.

DOREEN: Cathy White? (*She looks straight at JACK*) No … No, I don't know anyone of that name.

JACK: But surely you had dinner with her last night, at a restaurant in Greek Street?

DOREEN: (*Pleasantly*) No, I've just told you, I don't know anyone called Cathy … White. Sorry. (*Taking PENN's arm*) Come on, duckie – I'm getting hungry.

PENN looks at JACK, is about to say something, then gives a friendly nod and goes out with DOREEN. JACK stands for a moment, staring at the door, then he crosses to the bar and sits on one of the stools.

JACK: A scotch and soda, please.

CECIL: Yes, sir. Excuse me, sir – Mr Kerry?

JACK: Yes.

CECIL: There's been a phone message for you, sir, from a
           Mrs Lincoln. She's very sorry, she won't be able to
           keep her appointment with you after all.

JACK: (*Annoyed*) When was this – when did she phone?

CECIL: Oh – about half an hour ago, sir.

JACK: Did she say anything else?

CECIL: Yes; she said she'd phone you later tonight, sir – at
           your flat.

JACK: I see. Thank you.

CECIL: Scotch and soda, you said, sir?

JACK: Yes. No ice.

CUT TO: The Front Door of JACK KERRY's Flat. Night.
*JACK arrives home from The Golden Plough. As he crosses
from the staircase to the front door, he suddenly becomes
aware of the fact that the telephone is ringing inside the flat.
He quickly takes out his keys and opens the door.*

CUT TO: The Living Room of JACK KERRY's Flat. Night.
*JACK enters from the hall and swiftly crosses to the telephone,
which is still ringing – as he reaches the desk and picks up the
receiver it stops.*

JACK: (*On the phone*) Hello? … Mrs Lincoln? … Hello?
           … Hello? …

*JACK looks at the telephone, hesitates, then taps the receiver
– immediately he does so the dialling tone starts.*

JACK: Oh, damn!

*JACK replaces the receiver and stands by the desk looking
down at the telephone. It suddenly starts ringing again, and he
snatches up the receiver. The dialling tone returns. With a
gesture of annoyance, JACK replaces the receiver and takes off
his overcoat. He tosses the coat down on to the settee, looks at
the telephone – as if expecting it to ring again at any moment
– then crosses towards the bedroom.*

CUT TO: JACK KERRY's Bedroom. Night.

This is a small bedroom furnished with period furniture. It has an untidy masculine look about it, but is not in any way a dark or depressing room. There are several photographs, and family souvenirs, on the dressing table and mantelpiece.

JACK enters from the living room, taking his dressing gown off a hook on the door as he does so. He turns towards the wardrobe, then suddenly freezes – staring into the full-length mirror on the door of the wardrobe. The camera tracks in to a close-up of the wardrobe – in the mirror we see the body of FREDA LINCOLN. The dead woman is lying across the bed, a knife between her ribs.

END OF EPISODE THREE

EPISODE FOUR

OPEN TO: The Living Room of JACK KERRY's Flat. Night. *JACK is now sitting on the settee talking to BROMFORD; he appears worried and on edge and as he talks, he occasionally turns and looks nervously towards the bedroom. The bedroom door is open, and we can see ED ROYCE, together with a group of plain-clothes men, examining the contents of the room – taking fingerprints, photographs, etc. BROMFORD, as usual, seems rather bad tempered.*

JACK: … If you don't believe me – if you don't believe a word I say – there seems to be very little point in my telling you anything!

BROMFORD: Now wait a minute, let's get this straight. I'm not disputing the fact that you went to this pub – in any case your story can be checked with the barman and this other man you saw, Penn – but what I don't understand, is why you had to go there in the first place?

JACK: But I've told you why I went there – to see Mrs Lincoln.

BROMFORD: But why didn't she come here, to the flat – what was the point of meeting in a pub in St John's Wood?

JACK: (*Trying to control himself*) I don't know. The pub was her idea, not mine.

BROMFORD: (*After a moment; a shade too pleasant*) You asked her to come here and she refused, so you arranged to meet her in the saloon bar at The Golden Plough. That's your story, Kerry?

JACK: That's what happened, sir, it's not just my story.

ED joins them.

ED: (*To JACK*) Now you're certain – absolutely certain – that you didn't touch the body?

JACK: (*Shaking his head*) I didn't touch anything; I didn't go near the bed.

ED: Good. Now what about relatives – next of kin? Is there a Mr Lincoln?

JACK: No; he died about ten years ago. She had no family; but there's a nephew – Leonard Lincoln. He works for the Storm Insurance Company.

BROMFORD: In London?

JACK: Yes, I think so.

BROMFORD: (*To ED*) All right, leave that to me. (*He looks at his watch*) Good heavens, we've been here nearly two hours! I'll see you in the morning, Ed.

ED: Yes, sir.

BROMFORD nods to JACK and goes out.

JACK: (*After a moment: quietly*) He doesn't believe me, Ed. He just doesn't believe a single word I say!

JACK and ED look at each other. ED appears to be worried, puzzled.

CUT TO: The Front door of JACK KERRY's Flat. Later that night.

LEONARD LINCOLN is standing in front of the door, pressing the bell. He wears grey flannel trousers with a polo necked sweater and has obviously dressed in a hurry. The door opens almost immediately, and JACK appears. He has a drink in his hand and looks tired and drawn.

JACK: Come in, Mr Lincoln, I've been expecting you.

LEONARD: Kerry, is this true – about my aunt? Is it really true?

JACK: Yes, I'm afraid it is. Please come in …

LEONARD enters the hall.

98

LEONARD: My God, I just can't believe it … A man called Bromford – Superintendent Bromford – came to see me … A big chap.

JACK: (*Closing the door*) Yes, I know.

LEONARD: I was in bed … I make a point of having one early night a week and … (*Taking hold of JACK's arm*) Kerry, what happened? What the hell happened?

JACK: (*Quietly*) Come into the living room – let me get you a drink.

CUT TO: The Living Room of JACK KERRY's Flat. Night.

JACK enters followed by LEONARD LINCOLN. JACK crosses towards the drinks table.

JACK: What would you like?

LEONARD: Nothing … I don't drink … (*Tensely*) Kerry, what happened tonight?

JACK: (*Turning; putting down his drink*) Didn't the Superintendent tell you what happened?

LEONARD: He said you'd arranged to meet my aunt at a pub in St John's Wood. He said you kept the appointment, but she didn't turn up. Then, when you got back here, you found her in your bedroom – dead – murdered …

JACK: Yes, that's true, that's exactly what happened.

LEONARD: (*Bewildered*) But I just don't understand this! When I spoke to my aunt …

JACK: (*Interrupting LEONARD*) Lincoln, please sit down – there's something I want to say to you.

LEONARD hesitates, then sits in one of the armchairs. JACK moves across to him.

JACK: Your aunt and I never really hit if off together; I wasn't at all sorry when she decided to leave me.

To be frank, I never really liked her – and I don't think she liked me either. (*Facing LEONARD; shaking his head*) But I didn't kill her, Lincoln.

LEONARD: Good God, I never thought you did! It never entered my head! And you're absolutely wrong when you say my aunt didn't like you. She was very fond of you, Kerry – both you and your father. (*He rises*) But there's something I don't understand about tonight, something that just doesn't add up.

JACK: What do you mean?

LEONARD: This afternoon, she dropped in on me, unexpectedly. She said she'd spoken to you on the phone, you'd been charming to her, and that she was coming round here to see you.

JACK: (*Staggered*) She said she was coming here, to the flat?

LEONARD: Yes. She said you'd asked her round for a drink, some time this evening. The poor dear was really quite flattered.

JACK: But – but this isn't true!

LEONARD: That's what she told me, Kerry.

JACK: (*Alarmed*) Did – did you tell the Superintendent this?

LEONARD: Yes, of course I did, my dear fellow! What else could I tell him?

JACK stares at LEONARD LINCOLN.

CUT TO: The Box Room: JACK KERRY's Flat. Morning.
DOUGLAS comes quickly up the spiral staircase from the office below and crosses to the door. He is wearing outdoor clothes.

CUT TO: The Living Room of JACK KERRY's Flat. Morning.

JACK, wearing a dressing gown over pyjamas, is sitting at the table drinking a glass of milk. There is a newspaper propped up in front of him, but although he is staring at the paper it is obvious that his thoughts have wandered. There is a knock on the box room door and DOUGLAS appears.

JACK: (*Turning*) Hello, Douglas, you're early this morning. I take it you've heard the news?

DOUGLAS: Yes … Jack, this is terrible!

JACK: When did you hear about it?

DOUGLAS: About an hour ago. We were having breakfast and suddenly your friend Ed Royce dropped in on us. My God, he's a different chap when he's on the job, isn't he? You'll hardly believe it, he questioned me for half an hour.

JACK: I believe it.

DOUGLAS: When did I first meet Mrs Lincoln? When did I last see her? What sort of woman was she? Did I get on with her? (*Shaking his head*) Phew!

JACK: (*Quietly*) Sit down, Doug. I'm sorry I can't offer you a cup of coffee, I didn't feel like making any this morning.

DOUGLAS: (*Hesitantly*) Jack, I know it's none of my business, but …

JACK: Sit down …

DOUGLAS hesitates, then sits at the table.

DOUGLAS: Jack, do you think this murder – and the Delaney affair – do you think they've anything to do with – what happened to your father?

JACK: Yes, I do. (*Quietly; facing DOUGLAS*) What's on your mind, Doug? What is it you want to tell me?

DOUGLAS: I know something about your father; I don't honestly think it's got anything to do with this business, but – (*Shaking his head*) I swore I wouldn't say anything about it. I promised him that …

JACK: What is it, Doug?

DOUGLAS: Your father was having an affair with someone – a married woman. I discovered it quite by accident. I went down to Worthing one weekend, and they were staying at the same hotel.

JACK: Go on …

DOUGLAS: Your father ignored me the whole of that weekend, it was just as if he'd never seen me before. Then, in the office on the Monday morning, he told me all about it. He said he'd known this woman for some little time – she was married, her husband was an invalid, and there could never be any question of a divorce. He asked me to say nothing about the affair, to you, or anyone else. Naturally, I agreed.

JACK: Did he tell you who his friend was?

DOUGLAS: No, he simply referred to her as Iris. But her name's Bannister, I've discovered that since.

JACK: (*Quietly*) How? How did you discover her name was Bannister?

DOUGLAS: She telephoned me.

JACK: When?

DOUGLAS: The day before yesterday. She said although we'd never met, she'd heard all about me from your father. She wanted to know whether I could help her at all.

JACK: Help her – in what way?

DOUGLAS: Well, apparently while she was out with your father one night her pearl necklace broke. Your father sent it away to be restrung and she hasn't the slightest idea where he sent it. She wondered if I could find the receipt.

JACK: Have you found it?

DOUGLAS: No; it's not in the office, certainly not in his desk.

JACK: Supposing you had found it? What did she want you to do with it?

DOUGLAS: She asked me to post it to an hotel in Aldeburgh.

JACK: I see. Is that why you borrowed the A.A. book from Liz?

DOUGLAS: (*Puzzled by the question*) Yes. Mrs Bannister told me the name of the hotel and I promptly forgot it. I remembered it, of course, when I saw it in the book.

The door bell rings.

JACK: Thank you, Doug. I'm glad you told me this.

DOUGLAS: Well, in view of what's happened, I thought it only fair that ... (*He looks towards the hall*)

JACK: Excuse me.

JACK rises and goes out into the hall. DOUGLAS gets up from the table and thoughtfully takes out a packet of cigarettes. He is thinking of his conversation with JACK. Suddenly, he hears voices, and turns towards the hall. He puts the packet of cigarettes back in his pocket as JACK returns with ED and SUPERINTENDENT BROMFORD.

ED: Hello, Mr Croft! We meet again!

DOUGLAS: (*Quietly*) Good morning.

JACK: (*To BROMFORD*) This is Douglas Croft, he's been running the shop for me since my father died.

103

BROMFORD: (*Interrupting JACK, not interested*) Yes, I know. Good morning, sir.

DOUGLAS: Good morning. (*To JACK*) If you'll excuse me, I've rather a lot to do this morning.

JACK: Yes, of course.

DOUGLAS: We'll probably see you later, Jack?

JACK: Yes, and thank you, Doug.

DOUGLAS nods to ED and the SUPERINTENDENT and goes into the box room.

BROMFORD: (*To JACK*) May I sit down?

JACK: Yes, of course, sir.

BROMFORD: My feet are killing me this morning. (*He sits in an armchair*) You always hear these corny old jokes about policemen and their feet, but by God they're true! (*He looks at JACK*) I saw Mr Lincoln last night – the nephew.

JACK: Yes, I know. I've seen him too.

BROMFORD: Then you know about the phone call, the one he had from his aunt?

JACK: Yes. (*A moment*) It's not true, sir.

BROMFORD looks at JACK, then at ED.

ED: You mean, you don't believe Lincoln? You don't think his aunt did phone and tell him …

JACK: (*Interrupting ED*) Yes, I think she phoned him, and I think she told him she was coming here, but – (*He shakes his head*) she wasn't telling the truth.

BROMFORD: Why should she lie about a thing like that?

JACK: I don't know, sir. I wish I did. But she did lie, and we've got proof of it.

ED: Proof, Jack?

JACK: Yes, she telephoned the pub and left a message for me. Why should she do that if we'd arranged to meet here in the first place?

104

BROMFORD: <u>Someone</u> telephoned the pub and left a message, Kerry. We don't know for certain that it was Mrs Lincoln.

The telephone rings.

ED: The barman didn't know her, it was just a voice on the phone, so far as he was concerned.

JACK: Yes, I know, Ed, but if we're going to doubt every ...

JACK breaks off and, somewhat irritated, crosses to the desk and picks up the phone.

JACK: (*On the phone*) Hello? ... Yes, speaking ... Yes, he's here, he's just arrived ... (*To ED*) It's your office ...

ED: May I take it in the bedroom?

JACK: (*Faintly surprised*) Yes, of course.

ED goes into the bedroom. JACK holds the receiver for a moment, looking across at BROMFORD; when he hears ED's voice, he replaces the receiver.

BROMFORD: Kerry, I think if I remember rightly, you told me that Mrs Lincoln was <u>working</u> at the Royal Plaza.

JACK: Yes, that's what she said.

BROMFORD: (*Shaking his head*) She was staying there, as a guest. She had a room on the tenth floor, she'd booked it for five weeks. It was costing her three pounds fifteen a day, without meals.

JACK: But how on earth could Mrs Lincoln afford to pay that sort of money?

BROMFORD: I don't know.

JACK: Does her nephew know about this?

BROMFORD: He does now. Ed told him this morning.

JACK: What did he say?

BROMFORD: He was puzzled – very puzzled. Like you, he was under the impression his aunt was working at the hotel.

JACK: (*Puzzled*) I don't understand this. I'm damned if I do!

BROMFORD: Neither do I. (*He rises*) But then, there's lots of things I don't understand. (*Quietly*) I wish to God you'd put me in the picture, Kerry.

JACK: (*Surprised*) Me?

BROMFORD: Yes, you. (*Facing JACK*) In my opinion you're holding out on me. You haven't told me the truth. You haven't told me the truth about anything.

JACK: I told you the truth about the Bannisters – and what happened? You didn't believe me.

BROMFORD: How could I believe you when the Bannisters denied the story and your cheque was found on Delaney? And all that damn nonsense about Charles Bannister and a wheelchair! When I spoke to Inspector Everson about it, he laughed himself silly.

JACK: Nevertheless, it was the truth! (*Looking at BROMFORD*) And I'll tell you something else about the Bannisters – something else you won't believe.

BROMFORD: (*Quietly; looking at JACK*) Go on.

JACK: (*After a pause*) She was having an affair with my father.

BROMFORD: Mrs Bannister was?

JACK: Yes.

BROMFORD: Who told you this?

JACK: Doug – Douglas Croft. He went down to Worthing one weekend and my father and Iris Bannister were staying at the same hotel.

BROMFORD: Is he sure about this?

JACK: Yes; and so am I. There's no doubt about it.

BROMFORD: Did Croft actually meet Mrs Bannister – were they introduced to each other?

JACK: No, but she phoned him the other day about a pearl necklace my father was supposed to be having restrung for her. She didn't know what had happened to it and she thought perhaps the receipt was in the office and Douglas could get it for her.

BROMFORD: Was it in the office?

JACK: No, it wasn't.

BROMFORD: (*Thoughtfully*) Kerry, do you think Mrs Lincoln knew about this – about your father and Mrs Bannister?

JACK: Yes. Yes, I do …

BROMFORD nods, he stands for a moment, deep in thought. ED comes out of the bedroom.

ED: (*To BROMFORD*) Excuse me, sir.

BROMFORD: (*Turning*) Yes, what is it, Ed?

ED: There's been a message from Hampstead – from Inspector Everson.

BROMFORD: Dick Everson? What does he want?

ED: Well, I only got the message second hand, sir – but I gather he wants to talk to you. (*He looks at JACK*) About a wheelchair …

CUT TO: Outside Hampstead Police Station. Morning.
CHARLES BANNISTER's Bentley is parked outside the station. CHARLES and IRIS BANNISTER emerge from the building and cross towards the car; they look depressed and appear to be in rather a bad mood with each other. As the Bentley drives away it passes a police car which is drawing into the kerb. BROMFORD gets out of the police car and looks

across at the Bentley which he has recognised. After a moment, he turns and goes into the building.

CUT TO: INSPECTOR EVERSON's Office, Hampstead Police Station. Morning.

EVERSON is sitting behind his desk writing a letter; he is a thick-set, pleasant looking man in his late fifties. There is a knock, the door opens, and BROMFORD pops his head into the room.

BROMFORD: Is everybody dead around here, or is it the coffee break?

EVERSON: Hello, Hal! (*He rises and comes round the desk*) Come along in! Nice to see you.

BROMFORD and EVERSON shake hands; it is obvious they are old friends.

EVERSON: Sit down, Hal. Would you like some coffee?

BROMFORD: I'd love a cup of tea.

EVERSON: Good idea.

EVERSON picks up the intercom phone and presses a button.

EVERSON: Baker, we want some tea, straight away ... No, tea – and wipe that grin off your face. (*Smiling*) I don't have to see it.

EVERSON replaces the phone. BROMFORD sits in the armchair.

BROMFORD: I got your message, Dick. What's it all about?

EVERSON: Something happened last night, or rather early this morning, which I thought might interest you.

BROMFORD: Something to do with the Bannisters?

EVERSON: Yes.

BROMFORD: I thought so. I've just seen them, they were driving away as I arrived.

EVERSON: (*Nodding*) Yes; that's right.

BROMFORD: Well, what is it, Dick? What's happened?

EVERSON: Their house was broken into, and in spite of the fact that there was quite a lot of stuff there – pretty valuable stuff I should say – nothing was taken. (*Suddenly, correcting himself*) No, I'm sorry, that's not strictly true – a pearl necklace was stolen, belonging to Mrs Bannister, but that's all.

BROMFORD: When did this happen?

EVERSON: About half past one this morning. The Bannisters were away, they were down at Aldeburgh ...

BROMFORD: Yes, they told me they were going there.

EVERSON: ... One of our chaps noticed that the front gate was open, and since we've had one or two break-ins just recently, he decided to take a look round. To cut a long story short, the place had been ransacked. But it was utterly impossible of course for us to tell whether anything was missing. I telephoned the Bannisters and they arrived home – not in the best of tempers, I might add – at about four o'clock.

BROMFORD: Go on, Dick.

EVERSON: Now this is the curious point, and this is why I sent for you. When I first went over the house, at about two o'clock, I saw something in one of the bedrooms which – in view of our recent conversation – immediately aroused my curiosity. I don't have to tell you what it was.

BROMFORD: A wheelchair?

EVERSON: (*Nodding*) Right. The chair was in a cupboard, a sort of built-in wardrobe, the door of which has been broken open. (*He takes out his pipe and pouch*) Well, the Bannisters arrived home and at about half past eight I drove down there again. Things were still a bit higgledy-piggledy, but they'd done quite a bit of tidying up considering the mess they were in. They both said that, so far as they could tell, nothing was missing. It was on the tip of my tongue to mention the chair and then suddenly, for some reason or other, I don't know why, I changed my mind and asked Bannister if I could look over the house again. He agreed and for about fifteen minutes we wandered all over the place.

BROMFORD: Did you go into the bedroom, the one with –

EVERSON: Yes, we did. We went into the bedroom, and I made a point of showing him the cupboard. (*Looking at BROMFORD*) The chair wasn't there, it had gone.

BROMFORD: Gone?

EVERSON: (*Nodding*) Yes, it had disappeared. Obviously, someone had taken it away, and taken it away after the burglary, after I'd seen it, in fact.

BROMFORD: Did you make any comment?

EVERSON: Not about the chair. I simply asked Bannister to take a good look inside the cupboard and tell me if anything was missing. He said, "No, everything's just the same, Inspector. Nothing's been taken". Those were his exact words.

BROMFORD: Thank you, Dick. Now tell me about the pearl necklace.

EVERSON: Well, that's a new development. I've only just heard about it myself. The Bannisters dropped in on me about fifteen minutes ago. Mrs Bannister said she'd now discovered a pearl necklace had been stolen and she gave me a description of it. I must admit it seemed a little odd to me that someone should break into a house – a house full of very valuable things – and just pinch a pearl necklace.

BROMFORD: Did she say how much the necklace was worth?

EVERSON: Yes, about three hundred pounds. (*Picking up a box of matches*) But it's the wheelchair that puzzles me.

BROMFORD: (*Thoughtfully*) You're not the only one, Dick.

CUT TO: NORMAN PENN's Pet Shop, St John's Wood, London. Morning.

NORMAN PENN is saying an effusive goodbye to a middle-aged woman who, loaded with parcels, is making a hasty retreat. JACK enters and with a brief nod crosses to the counter – as the door closes behind the customer. PENN quickly turns and joins JACK.

JACK: Good morning.

PENN: Good morning, Mr Kerry! I've been expecting you. I thought you'd be dropping in on me some time this morning.

JACK: I take it you've already seen a colleague of mine?

PENN: Yes; Superintendent Bromford, I think he said his name was, he called very early, before I was open in fact. He wanted to know if I'd seen you last night.

JACK: And what did you tell him?

PENN: I told him I had, of course. I said we'd bumped into each other at The Plough. (*Puzzled*) But what's this all about, Mr Kerry? He said it was something to do with your housekeeper, but he was frightfully evasive.

111

JACK: Mrs Lincoln, my housekeeper – or rather my ex-housekeeper – was found murdered last night.

PENN: Murdered! Good God! Where? Where did it happen?

JACK: In my flat …

PENN: But what an appalling thing! Have you any idea who …

JACK: (*Interrupting PENN*) Mr Penn, forgive me, I'm in rather a hurry this morning, and I've one or two questions I'd like to ask you.

PENN: By all means – anything I can do to help you, Mr Kerry.

JACK: Then, would you mind telling me who that girl was – the girl I saw you with last night.

PENN: (*Embarrassed*) Oh dear … Oh dear, I do wish you hadn't asked that question. Her name's Doreen Osborne.

JACK: Is she a friend of yours?

PENN: Good gracious, no. I assure you most of my friends are … Well, we've bumped into each other from time to time, if that's what you mean. Usually in the local.

JACK: Tell me all you know about her.

PENN: I really don't know anything about her.

JACK: (*With authority*) Mr Penn, I'm investigating a murder case. I want you to tell me all you know about Doreen Osborne.

PENN: (*Looking at JACK, hesitating*) I – I first saw her about three months ago, in The Plough. She was cadging drinks and making eyes at everyone and … (*Shuddering*) Oh dear – I thought she was a dreadful person.

JACK: Go on …

PENN: Well, about a month ago she came in here and bought a cat. The Siamese cat you saw last night. She's been popping in and out ever since, sometimes she spends a great deal of money with me.

JACK: Is she well off?

PENN: Well – at the moment she seems to have money to burn. But when I first saw her, she – I told you, she was always playing up to people, cadging drinks.

JACK: Have you met a friend of hers called Cathy White?

PENN: No, never. But then I wouldn't, I don't know any of her friends. I've just told you, Doreen's not really a friend of mine.

JACK: But you had dinner together last night.

PENN: Yes, we did last night, but … Well, it was really awkward, Mr Kerry. You see, the day before she'd been in here and spent quite a lot of money, and when I met her in The Plough last night, she started talking about a little restaurant in Baker Street and – well, before I knew what had happened we'd arranged to have dinner there.

JACK: (*Quietly*) Where does she live?

PENN: (*A shade surprised by the question*) Where – does she live?

JACK: Yes.

PENN: She has a flat in Defoe Mansions.

JACK: Where's that?

PENN: It's on the Carrington Road.

JACK: Have you been there?

PENN: No, never. Well – once.

JACK looks at PENN.

PENN: Twice, as a matter of fact.

JACK: What number Defoe Mansions?

PENN: Thirty-two, I think it is. Yes, thirty-two …

JACK: Thank you, Mr Penn.

JACK turns and goes out of the shop. PENN stands, faintly embarrassed, looking towards the door.

CUT TO: Defoe Mansions: A block of flats on the Carrington Road, London, N.W.8. Morning.

Defoe Mansions was originally three dilapidated houses. They have now been converted, not very skilfully, into so-called "Luxury" flats.

CLEG REED walks out of the building towards a phone box on the corner of the road. He wears a new sports jacket and is smoking a cigar.

The Austin 1100 draws up and JACK gets out of it, looking up at the name above the entrance to the flats as he does so. CLEG recognises JACK and is obviously surprised to see him. JACK realises that he is being stared at by an apparent stranger and looks across at CLEG with interest. CLEG tosses the cigar butt into the road and continues towards the phone box. JACK goes into the building.

CLEG reaches the phone box, turns and looks back at the block of flats, then enters the box.

CUT TO: Inside the Telephone Box. Morning.

CLEG is dialling a number, after a moment we hear it ringing out at the other end. It rings for a little while and then a man's voice comes on the line; CLEG holds the receiver close to his ear and stares out into the street. We can hardly hear the voice.

CLEG: …Mel? … This is Cleg … Listen, I'm outside Doreen's place, I've just delivered the passport … No, no, she's okay – but listen to this! I've just seen Jack Kerry … No, two minutes ago … Yes, he's just gone in there … Well, I hope she does play it cool … What? … This is a hell of a line!

... Yes, you do that, you phone her, that's a very good idea ... Okay, Mel ...

CUT TO: The Front Door of 32 Defoe Mansions. Morning.
JACK is standing in front of the door, his finger firmly planted on the bell. From inside the flat we hear the reaction to this – a series of musical chimes. After a moment, we hear a woman's voice calling: "All right – all right, I'm coming!" The door opens and JACK finds himself facing DOREEN OSBORNE. She wears a coat, carries a handbag, and is obviously just about to leave the flat.

DOREEN: For Gawd's sake, what are you trying ... (*She stops, recognising JACK*)

JACK: (*Pleasantly*) Good morning. My name's Kerry, Miss Osborne. Detective-Inspector Kerry. Could you spare me a few minutes?

DOREEN: (*Flustered*) Well – it's a bit awkward at the moment, I was just going out. I've got an appointment at the hairdresser's at half past eleven.

JACK: (*Smiling at DOREEN*) It'll only take a few minutes.

DOREEN: (*Hesitantly*) Well ...

JACK: You look to me as if you've just come back from the hairdresser's.

DOREEN is flustered and touches her hair.

DOREEN: Nonsense! It's all over the place – a frightful mess.

JACK: May I come in? Just for a moment.

DOREEN looks at her watch.

DOREEN: Yes, okay, but I warn you it will only have to be for a few minutes.

DOREEN opens the door wider and JACK enters the flat.

CUT TO: The Hall of the Flat. Morning.

The flat is over-furnished and over-heated. There is nothing simple or modest or homely about 32 Defoe Mansions – nothing to evoke sentimental twinges of conscience in the thoughts of tired businessmen. The whole apartment seems to have been furnished by someone with a passion for frills and cupids, glass doors and cupids. Gold doors, complete with wrought-iron cupids, open into the main lounge. Doors lead off the hall to kitchen, spare bedroom, bathroom, etc.

JACK: What a delightful flat!

DOREEN: (*Pleased*) Do you like it?

JACK: I do. I do indeed.

DOREEN and JACK cross into the living room.

CUT TO: The Living Room of the Flat. Morning.

The most important feature of this room is the large, ornate cocktail bar which occupies a complete corner of the living room. There is a divan, several chairs, and a centre table complete with drawers, telephones, etc. A door leads out of this room into the main bedroom.

After JACK has been in the room a little while he casually notices a woman's handbag – CATHY's – lying on the arm of one of the chairs.

DOREEN: I'm sorry I can't offer you a drink, there really isn't time …

JACK: Miss Osborne, I'll tell you why I wanted to see you …

DOREEN: I think I know why, duckie. Cathy White?

JACK: (*Surprised*) Yes …

DOREEN: I nearly phoned you last night, after I'd seen you in The Plough, and then I thought … You keep out of this, Doreen. Don't you get mixed up in anything. You've always been a good little girl –

116

	with reservations, of course – you keep it that way, sweetie.
JACK:	But you do know Cathy?
DOREEN:	Yes, of course I know her. Don't know her very well, but – she stayed the night with me, the night Delaney … died.
JACK:	Where is she now?
DOREEN:	I don't know, duckie. And that's the truth – honestly, I don't know.
JACK:	(*After a moment*) Look, I'm going to be frank with you. I'm in a spot, I've got to find Cathy White and I've got to find her before …
DOREEN:	Sweetie, I've just told you, I don't know where she is – I haven't a clue. I haven't seen her since she did a bunk that night.
JACK:	(*Looking at DOREEN*) Is that the truth?
DOREEN:	(*Crossing her bosom*) Cross my heart …

JACK, after a moment, apparently disappointed, yet giving DOREEN's arm an affectionate squeeze.

JACK:	Okay … Okay, I believe you.
DOREEN:	In any case, you're barking up the wrong tree. She didn't kill Delaney, he was her meal ticket, so why should she kill him?
JACK:	They had a row that night.
DOREEN:	So what? I'm always having rows, but I haven't knocked anybody off. Not yet.
JACK:	Did you know Delaney?
DOREEN:	Yes, I knew him. Didn't like him very much. Altogether too much of a smoothie for my liking. Always thought he was a bit of a queer, as a matter of fact; but he wasn't.
JACK:	Well – I'm sorry you can't help me. (*Nodding towards the bar*) And I'm sorry about the drink. Some other time, perhaps?

117

DOREEN: Why not? We're always open.

JACK: Open to offers?

DOREEN: I meant the bar. But we're open to offers too, sweetie.

JACK laughs and he and DOREEN cross towards the hall.

CUT TO: The Hall of the Flat.

JACK: I'll drop in again, if I may? One evening, perhaps – <u>after</u> you've been to the hairdresser's.

DOREEN: You do that, but give me a ring first. And I'm sorry I couldn't be more helpful – about Cathy, I mean. But you're wasting your time, you really are, duckie. (*Shaking her head*) She didn't kill Delaney.

The telephone rings in the living room.

JACK: Then who did?

DOREEN: I don't know, but it certainly wasn't Cathy. See you.

JACK nods and opens the front door. DOREEN returns to the living room. JACK quickly puts the door on the latch, then goes out, closing the door behind him.

CUT TO: The Living Room of the Flat.

DOREEN crosses to the table and picks up the phone.

DOREEN: (*On the phone*) Hello? … Yes … Wait a minute!

DOREEN puts the receiver down on the table, then quickly crosses the room again and looks out into the hall. It is empty and the front door closed – obviously satisfied, DOREEN returns to the phone.

CUT TO: Outside the Front Door. Morning.

JACK is standing close to the door, listening to DOREEN's voice on the phone inside the flat. It is impossible to hear what she is saying. JACK slowly pushes the door open and re-enters the hall, then quietly closes the door and releases the lock. From the living room we hear DOREEN's voice on the phone:

118

DOREEN's VOICE: … He's just left … Yes, I did … It would have looked a hell of a lot fishier if I hadn't asked him in … No, I played it cool … What? … Well, she's all right, but she's nervous … Yes, I think it's very good, the photograph's excellent … No, he didn't, I'm picking the ticket up myself … Mel, listen … (*Pleading*) Do you always have to send Cleg? Couldn't it be someone else, just for once …? (*Horrified*) Like him? He's a flaming monster!

JACK stands listening to DOREEN – suddenly he realises that the phone conversation is nearly at an end, and he quickly opens one of the doors in the hall and slips into an adjoining room.

CUT TO: The Living Room of the Flat
DOREEN is finishing her phone conversation.
DOREEN: … All right, I'll do that … No, there's no need. And, Mel, remember what I said about Cleg … Yes, I will … Bye …

DOREEN replaces the phone and picks up her handbag.

CUT TO: The Hall of the Flat.
DOREEN enters the hall and crosses to the front door: she is now searching her handbag for something – obviously not finding the article she is looking for, she turns towards the room where JACK is hiding. Just as she reaches the door, she stops, having finally discovered her lipstick at the bottom of her handbag. She turns and goes out of the flat. After a moment, JACK's door opens, and he comes into the hall. He glances at the front door, then quickly crosses towards the living room.

119

CUT TO: The Living Room of the Flat.

JACK enters and crosses to the table. He stands looking around the room – noticing, amongst other things, CATHY's handbag which is still on the arm of the chair. After a second or two, he turns his attention to the table, scrutinising the address book by the side of the telephone, opening the drawers and looking at the contents. He discovers a passport in one of the drawers and carefully examines it. The passport is made out to a Miss Stella Morgan, the photograph is that of CATHY WHITE, a distinguished CATHY wearing glasses and a completely different hairstyle.

JACK is looking at the passport when suddenly, instinctively, he becomes aware of the fact that he is being watched and he slowly turns and looks towards the bedroom. CATHY WHITE is standing in the doorway: a pale, tense, worried looking girl, her hair done in the style registered in the passport. She is wearing a dressing-gown and holds a gun in her hand.

JACK: (*Quietly, obviously not taken by surprise*) Hello, Cathy. How's life?

CATHY doesn't answer.

JACK: Not too good by the look of things. (*He indicates the handbag*) You're getting careless in your old age.

CATHY still doesn't answer. JACK looks at the passport.

JACK: It's not a very good photograph, is it? Still, it's not a very good passport either, if it comes to that. (*He looks up*) Who got you this useless piece of cardboard, Cathy? Mel Harris?

CATHY: (*Tensely*) Give it to me.

JACK: Sure.

JACK tosses the passport onto the table. CATHY moves down to the table and picks it up: the gun still pointing at JACK.

JACK: Do you know what I'd do with that, if I were you? I'd burn it.

CATHY: I'm not interested in what you'd do with it.

JACK: (*Moving nearer to CATHY*) Aren't you, Cathy? (*He points to the gun*) Is that the gun you shot Delaney with?

CATHY: I didn't shoot Rupert!

JACK: Then why are you running away?

CATHY: Don't you know why?

JACK: Yes, I know. You're running away because someone's convinced you we're going to charge you with this murder – whether you did it or not. (*Shaking his head*) It isn't true, Cathy. I told you that the other night, if you tell the truth, you've nothing to worry about.

CATHY: I don't believe you! Even if you believed my story, Ed Royce wouldn't.

JACK: (*Puzzled*) Why shouldn't Ed believe you?

CATHY ignores the question and raises the gun.

CATHY: There's a room through the hall, on the right. I want you to go into it.

JACK: Cathy, listen to me. I took a risk the other night when I …

CATHY: (*Tensely*) You heard what I said – go into the hall!

JACK looks at CATHY: for the first time he realises she might pull the trigger. After a moment, he backs towards the hall, CATHY following.

JACK: I hope you know what you're doing. If you use that passport and <u>then</u> we pick you up …

CATHY: (*Overwrought*) Do as I tell you – go into the hall.

JACK: (*Quietly*) All right, Cathy.

JACK half turns his back on CATHY, as if to follow her instructions to cross into the hall – then suddenly he springs forward with the intention of knocking the gun out of CATHY's hand.

CATHY is quickly aware of what is happening and backs away from JACK, keeping a firm grip on the gun. JACK's manoeuvre has failed, and he realises it – he also realises that he has no alternative but to come to grips with CATHY. He quickly grabs her arm and pulls her towards him, for a moment there is a violent struggle – then the gun explodes, and CATHY gives a sudden cry of pain. JACK is bewildered, desperately worried, as he holds CATHY in his arms …

JACK: (*Softly*) Oh, my God … Cathy …

END OF EPISODE FOUR

EPISODE FIVE

OPEN TO: A London Street. Morning.

An ambulance is racing through the London streets; bell ringing, "Accident" light flashing.

CUT TO: A London Hospital. Morning.

The entrance to the Casualty Department.

The ambulance pulls into a courtyard and stops opposite the door to the Casualty Department. Stretcher bearers jump out of the ambulance followed by JACK and a neatly dressed little man – DOCTOR HASLING. JACK watches CATHY being taken into the hospital, then turns towards the DOCTOR.

JACK: Are you sure she's going to be all right, doctor?

HASLING: Yes; don't worry, Inspector. I've told you, it's not serious; she's suffering from shock more than anything else.

JACK follows the DOCTOR into the hospital and as he does so a police car swerves into the courtyard and in a matter of seconds ED ROYCE has jumped out of the car and is racing into the building.

CUT TO: A Waiting Room in the Hospital. Morning.

JACK is standing with his back against a radiator, facing ED who is sitting straddle-legged on a wooden chair.

ED: For heaven's sake, relax! They've already told you she's going to be all right. My God, if I were you, I'd be out celebrating, instead of worrying about a little tramp that tried to shoot the hell out of me. (*He points to the door*) You could be out there, chum – don't you realise that? You could be out there lying on a slab for all she cares.

JACK: Yes, I know. I know that's what it must look like, Ed, but – (*Shaking his head*) I'm sorry, I don't share your opinion of this girl, I never have done.

125

ED: (*Amazed*) Jack, what is this? Are you falling for her?

JACK: Don't be a damn fool!

ED: (*Aggressively*) Well, are you? (*He gets off the chair*) Let me tell you something about this outfit, let me really put you in the picture. Ever since those photographs were found – the ones at Delaney's – I've been checking up on Mr Rupert Delaney and Miss Cathy White.

JACK looks at ED.

ED: Sergeant Quilter and I must have talked to half the prostitutes in London, to say nothing of the ponces. (*Touching his forehead*) We're up to here in sex, Jack, both of us. Right now, my idea of a swell night out would be a nice juicy apple and Mrs Dale's Diary.

JACK: (*Quietly*) What did you find out about Cathy?

ED: Delaney worked for a man called Mel Harris. Don't ask me who Mel Harris is because I don't know. Ostensibly, he runs a call-girl racket but in actual fact it's not quite as straight forward as that. A wealthy man comes to Town in search of fun and games; he calls a certain number and talks to Cathy White. She finds out who he is and passes him over to Rupert Delaney – or rather she did. Delaney provides the glamour pants and within twenty-four hours the poor sucker finds himself buying a very nice set of highly revealing photographs from our Mr Harris.

JACK: Yes, but aren't you forgetting something? It was Cathy who first told us about Mel Harris. Why should she do that if she was part of the game?

ED: It's pretty obvious why. She thought she had the skids under her, and she was frightened of you, Jack.

JACK: I don't agree. As a matter of fact, it's not me she's frightened of, Ed. It's you.

ED: (*Surprised*) Me? But I've never met the girl!

JACK: Never?

ED: No, never. What makes you think I have?

JACK: (*A shrug*) It's not important. The important thing is, where do we go from here?

ED: We've got to find Harris. But how, that's our problem? How do we get a lead on this bastard? And don't think Cathy White's going to talk, because she isn't. Harris has obviously put the fear of the devil into her.

JACK: (*Quietly*) There's always Doreen Osborne.

ED: You know what your friend Penn said about Miss Osborne – she's got money to burn. That money's coming from Mel Harris. (*Shaking his head*) She's not going to kill the golden goose, Jack.

JACK: (*Thoughtfully*) I wonder …

ED: (*Looking at JACK*) Well, if you think you made an impression on Miss Osborne – go ahead. Talk to her. Anything's worth a try.

The door opens and a young doctor – DOCTOR FRIEDMAN – enters with a uniformed nurse. He looks at JACK and ED.

FRIEDMAN: Inspector Kerry?

JACK: I'm Inspector Kerry.

FRIEDMAN: Miss White's been asking for you, sir –

JACK looks at ED.

FRIEDMAN: – but we've given her a sedative; it would be much better if you could call back later in the day.

JACK: How is she, doctor?

FRIEDMAN: Her arm's going to be perfectly all right, there's nothing to worry about there. But she's had a very nasty shock, I'm afraid. Anyway, we'll see how she is tonight. Could you make it fairly late, we'd like her to get as much sleep as possible.

JACK: You name the time, doctor.

FRIEDMAN: Would eight o'clock be convenient for you?

JACK: Yes – that's fine.

FRIEDMAN: Good.

JACK: Thank you, doctor.

The DOCTOR nods and goes out with the nurse.

ED: (*To JACK*) I'll meet you here at five to eight.

JACK nods, his thoughts elsewhere.

JACK: All right, Ed.

ED: I'm serious about Doreen Osborne, Jack. Give it a try …

CUT TO: Defoe Mansions, London, N.W.8. Late afternoon.

NORMAN PENN comes out of the block of flats and quickly crosses to a mini estate car which is parked near the kerb. He is agitated; almost, but not quite, in a panic. He has trouble opening the car door; eventually he succeeds and in a matter of seconds he is racing away in the mini.

The camera pans with the mini as it races down Carrington Road, and we see JACK KERRY standing by his car watching PENN make his hasty departure. It is obvious that JACK has just driven up and has been watching PENN for the last minute or two. As the mini disappears, JACK turns and walks towards Defoe Mansions.

CUT TO: The Front Door of 32 Defoe Mansions. Day.

JACK arrives and notices that the door is slightly ajar. A noise can be heard from inside the flat, but it is not immediately recognisable. Puzzled, JACK pushes the door open – hesitates, then steps into the hall.

CUT TO: The Hall of 32 Defoe Mansions. Day.
JACK stands in the hall listening to the noise, which is coming from the spare bedroom on the right, and which can now be identified as DOREEN sobbing. He crosses the hall and opens the bedroom door.

CUT TO: The Bedroom. Day.
DOREEN OSBORNE is sitting at a dressing table, dabbing her face with a towel and crying her eyes out. The reason is obvious – one has only to look at the torn dress she is wearing, the bruises on her bare shoulders, the ugly cuts on her face, to realise that she has recently been the victim of a vicious attack. JACK moves toward her and she slowly looks up at him.

DOREEN: (*Between sobs*) How the hell did you get in?

JACK: The door was open, and I heard you … You need a
            doctor!

JACK moves towards the phone.

DOREEN: (*Stopping JACK*) I don't want to see a doctor! I
            don't want to see anybody! (*Sobbing*) I don't ever
            want to see anybody again!

JACK: (*Quietly*) Who did this?

DOREEN: Please leave me alone …

JACK: Doreen, listen …

DOREEN: Didn't you hear what I said – leave me alone!

DOREEN continues to cry ad dab her face with the towel. JACK pulls up a bedside stool and sits next to her.

JACK: Doreen, I know who was responsible for this – you
            don't have to tell me.

DOREEN looks at JACK.

JACK: It was Mel Harris, wasn't it?

DOREEN: (*Hesitant; on the verge of a little nod*) … Oh, God, just look at me! Just look … My face! The swine …

JACK: Why did they do it? Because I found the passport – because you slipped up over Cathy?

DOREEN: Leave me alone! Please leave me alone …

JACK: Cathy's in hospital, did you know that?

DOREEN: (*Surprised*) In hospital?

JACK: Yes, there was an accident, she was shot.

DOREEN: (*Looking at JACK*) I don't believe you!

JACK: It's true. She's in Saint Matthew's.

DOREEN: Is – is she badly hurt?

JACK: No, no, I don't think so. I'm seeing her tonight. (*He points to DOREEN's face*) I know that looks pretty unsightly at the moment, but it's nowhere near as bad as you think it is. You find yourself a good doctor and inside a month there won't be a mark on you.

DOREEN: You're just saying that …

JACK: No, I'm not, honestly.

DOREEN looks in the mirror again and touches her face.

JACK: There's a plastic surgeon at Saint Matthew's, he's supposed to be a wizard. I think his name's Lathom, but I'm not sure. I'll find out for you tonight, if you like.

DOREEN: (*Softly*) Thanks …

JACK: (*After a moment, leaning towards DOREEN*) Doreen, you've got to tell me about Mel Harris. You've got to tell me who he is and how he …

DOREEN: (*Shaking her head*) Do you think I'm a fool! Can't you see what happened to me just because I was careless about Cathy, just because … I'm not telling you anything! (*Tensely, frightened*) In any case, I don't know what you're talking about. I don't know anyone called Mel Harris. (*She starts crying again*) Oh, God, my face! I look awful!

JACK: Sooner or later you'll have to tell me about Harris, you might just as well tell me now.

DOREEN: Please go away! Leave me alone!

JACK: What happened the night Delaney was murdered?

DOREEN: I don't know what happened. Cathy phoned me, she was in a terrible state, she asked me if she could stay the night here and I said she could … That's all I know … Now, please leave me alone! Please …

JACK: (*Rising*) All right, Doreen, we'll talk about this some other time. Is there anything you want? Anything I can do for you?

DOREEN: No. No, nothing. I'll have a couple of aspirin and go to bed for an hour.

JACK: Yes, that's a good idea. (*He nods and turns towards the door, then hesitates*) How long did Mr Penn stay with you?

DOREEN: Penn?

JACK: Yes.

DOREEN: (*Surprised*) I haven't seen Penn – he hasn't been here.

JACK: Hasn't he, Doreen? (*He looks at DOREEN for a moment, then:*) Don't you think you'd better lock the front door after me, just to be on the safe side?

DOREEN gives a little nod and follows JACK out into the hall.

CUT TO: NORMAN PENN's Pet Shop, St John's Wood. Late Afternoon.

The shop is closed but JACK can be seen outside, in the street, knocking on the door. After a little while, NORMAN PENN comes out of his office-cum-den and peers, somewhat short-sightedly, at the blurred figure of JACK seen through the glass panel of the door. JACK continues his knocking and with a

131

gesture of annoyance, PENN crosses and unbolts the shop door.

PENN: (*Opening the door*) We're closed! Can't you read the notice on … Oh, hello, Mr Kerry!

JACK: (*Walking into the shop*) I want to talk to you, Penn.

PENN: Yes – yes, of course. I'm afraid I didn't recognise you!

PENN closes the door and JACK moves towards the counter.

JACK: (*Turning, with authority*) What happened this afternoon?

PENN: This afternoon?

JACK: Yes – at Miss Osborne's?

PENN: (*Innocently*) I'm so sorry, I'm afraid I don't understand.

JACK: Then I'll spell it out for you. I want you to tell me, quite simply, what happened this afternoon when you went to Doreen Osborne's flat.

PENN: I think there's some mistake, Mr Kerry. I spent the entire afternoon, here, working on my accounts.

JACK: (*Shaking his head*) I saw you come out of Defoe Mansions. I saw you drive away. Now who did you see there and what happened?

PENN: I – I didn't see anyone. I … Oh dear, this is most embarrassing. I don't quite know what to say. I assure you, Mr Kerry, I'm not in the habit of visiting …

JACK: Look, Penn, let's get one thing straight. I'm not Doctor Kinsey, I'm a police officer. I'm not interested in your sex life. I don't care two hoots in hell who you sleep with, but there's one thing I want to know, and I want to know it now! What happened this afternoon?

PENN: (*Frightened*) May I – start at the beginning?

132

JACK: No! I don't want to hear the story of your life. I just want to know what happened this afternoon!

PENN: I – I went to Doreen's. It was about a quarter past five when I got there. I let myself into the flat and suddenly I heard a noise. I didn't realise what it was at first, and then … She was in the living room, on the floor, crying … My God, she looked awful … Her dress was torn and there was blood all over her face, and she … (*He covers his face with his hands*) She looked dreadful, Mr Kerry – really dreadful. I just didn't know what on earth to do.

JACK: What did you do?

PENN: I – I behaved very badly, I'm afraid. But do try and understand my position, Mr Kerry. There I was in a strange flat, with a strange woman, and …

JACK: You bolted.

PENN: Yes – yes, I'm afraid so.

JACK: Did Doreen see you?

PENN: I – I don't know; I honestly don't know whether she saw me or not.

JACK: You say you let yourself into the flat?

PENN: Yes; she gave me a key.

JACK: When?

PENN: Last night when we had dinner together. (*He takes the key out of his pocket*) She said if ever I felt like … having a drink with her … all I had to do was … (*He is embarrassed, lost for words*)

JACK: Is this the truth you've told me?

PENN: Yes. Yes, I swear it is, I wouldn't lie to you about a thing like this – honestly, I wouldn't. (*He looks at JACK*) You know me, Mr Kerry.

JACK: That's where you're wrong. I don't know you, Mr Penn. (*He takes the key out of PENN's hand*) I'll take the key.

133

JACK turns and walks out of the shop.

CUT TO: The Waiting Room in the Hospital. Night.
JACK and ED ROYCE are waiting for permission to see CATHY. ED is standing by the window, smoking a cigarette and talking to JACK who is sitting in an armchair.

ED: … I've never met Penn, it was Bromford who questioned him – but I must say his story sounds quite extraordinary to me.

JACK: Yes, but don't forget I did see him leave the flat, and he was frightened, almost in a panic in fact.

ED: Could he have been putting on an act?

JACK: Yes, I suppose so. But why should he?

ED: He'd just beaten her up, he was about to leave and then suddenly he spots you – so he pretends he's a frightened little man who hates violence and wouldn't hurt a fly.

JACK: It's possible, I suppose – but what's the motive? He's still got to have a motive.

ED: Maybe he's a kinky little guy and just did it for kicks. Girls like Doreen Osborne are frequently beaten up; it's a risk they take, it's all part of the game.

JACK: Yes, but there is another angle, of course.

ED: What's that?

JACK: Penn could be working for Harris.

ED: Yes, that's possible.

JACK: Or, alternatively, perhaps you're right after all, perhaps he is putting on an act, perhaps he's putting on a very big one.

ED: (*Looking at JACK*) What do you mean?

JACK: Maybe Penn's the man we're looking for, maybe he is Mel Harris.

ED: (*Obviously a shade taken aback by the suggestion*) Well – that's possible, I suppose.

ED stands for a moment looking at his cigarette, considering the possibility.

JACK: Ed, I've been thinking about this girl, Cathy White. If she does talk – if she is prepared to help us – we've got to take care of her. We can't just let her leave here and fend for herself, especially after what happened this afternoon to Doreen Osborne.

ED: I agree, but – (*Looking up*) What have you got in mind, Jack?

JACK: Some friends of mine have a hotel in the Cotswolds; it's quiet, hidden away. No one would ever know she was staying there.

ED: Where is this place?

JACK: I've told you – it's in the Cotswolds; a village called Steeple Aston. I don't suppose you've heard of it.

ED: No, I haven't. (*He looks at JACK*) Okay – if she talks, you have my permission to take her down there. But if she doesn't talk, then so far as I'm concerned, she's got to face up to …

ED stops as the door opens. DOCTOR FRIEDMAN enters.

FRIEDMAN: Good evening …

JACK: Good evening, Doctor.

ED: How's the patient this evening?

FRIEDMAN: Oh, she's quite a bit better. She can leave us tomorrow morning if she wants to. But she'll have to take it easy for the next few days. (*To JACK*) Mr Kerry, I told her you were here, and she said she'd very much like to see you, but – I gather she'd like to see you alone, if that's possible.

JACK looks at ED.

ED: That's okay, you go ahead, Jack. I'll wait.

JACK gives ED a nod and follows the DOCTOR out into the corridor.

CUT TO: A Private Room in the Hospital. Night.
CATHY is sitting in an armchair by the bed, smoking a cigarette. She is dressed, her arm is in a sling, and she looks pale. There is a knock and then the door opens, and JACK appears.

JACK: May I come in?
CATHY looks at JACK and gives a little nod.
JACK: (*Closing the door*) How do you feel?
CATHY: Not – not too bad …
JACK: Is the arm painful?
CATHY: No; it's all right at the moment.
JACK: I'm awfully sorry about what happened. I – I didn't mean to hurt you.
CATHY: It was my fault. I behaved stupidly. I realise that now. What – what are you going to do with me? What's going to happen?
JACK moves down to CATHY and pulls up a stool from the side of the bed.
JACK: (*Sitting down*) Cathy, I've got something to tell you. Doreen Osborne's been hurt – she's been beaten up by someone …
CATHY: No! Oh no! … When did this happen?
JACK: This afternoon. It's not very serious … but her face is marked, I'm afraid … (*Leaning forward*) Now listen, you've got to tell me the truth – I want to know the truth about Delaney and Mel Harris …
CATHY: But I told you the truth!
JACK: You said Rupert Delaney was in the property business – he wasn't. He and Mel Harris were running a call-girl set-up.

136

CATHY: (*A moment, then nodding*) Yes, I know. Doreen told me.

CATHY rises and stubs out her cigarette.

CATHY: She told me the whole story. I didn't know a thing about it, not until she … Oh, what's the use! … What's the use, you won't believe me anyway.

JACK: Tell me the story, then I'll tell you whether I believe you or not.

CATHY: According to Doreen, when Rupert first met me, he intended that I should work for him, that's why he brought me to London. Then, when I'd been here a little while, he fell for me and decided that … (*Shaking her head; tensely*) I knew nothing about this call-girl business. Rupert kept it from me – kept it from me completely. I knew absolutely nothing about it.

JACK: (*Looking at CATHY*) Is that the truth?

CATHY: Yes, it is.

JACK: But you knew about Doreen; you must have known the sort of life she was leading, otherwise …

CATHY: Yes, I knew about her. I knew all about her because … she was a friend of mine … But I swear to you, I didn't know about Rupert.

JACK: (*After a moment*) What happened the night I picked you up and took you back to my flat?

CATHY: Mel Harris knew that the police were looking for me and he got one of his girls to tip you off. Later that evening, when Doreen realised what had happened, she decided to help me. She told Mel Harris that Rupert had given me a letter – a letter containing information about him.

JACK: About Mel Harris?

CATHY: Yes.

JACK: Was it true – about the letter?

CATHY: No, but it did the trick. Harris was frightened I'd hand the letter over to the police. You know what happened.

JACK: He got cold feet, "rescued" you, and talked you into leaving the country?

CATHY: Yes; except that it was Doreen who did the talking. I've never met Mel Harris.

JACK: Never?

CATHY: No, never.

JACK: Wasn't it Harris who came to my flat that night – who knocked me out?

CATHY: No, it was a man called Cleg Reed. He's a friend of Doreen's – although "friend" is hardly the right word. I don't think he's a friend of anyone's.

JACK: Go on, Cathy …

CATHY: Doreen said if I stayed in this country I hadn't a chance. She said I'd already behaved suspiciously, and the police were bound to arrest me sooner or later … She promised to get me a false passport.

JACK: Through Mel Harris?

CATHY: Well – from Cleg Reed, but it was done through Harris.

JACK hesitates, then rises.

JACK: Cathy, I've asked you this question before, but I'm going to ask you it again. Did you kill Delaney?

CATHY: No, I didn't.

JACK: You didn't find out about him?

CATHY: What do you mean?

JACK: You didn't find out what he was up to, and suddenly take the law into your own hands?

CATHY: No, I didn't! It wasn't like that – it wasn't a bit like that! I wanted to help Rupert. I knew he was in trouble, and I was trying to persuade him to go to

138

the police about it. That's why we had that row that night in the restaurant …

JACK: But I thought you told me the row was about a dog collar …?

CATHY: It was – it was about the collar and the note. The one you received the morning after he was murdered …

JACK: (*Looking at CATHY; quietly*) Tell me about it, Cathy …

CUT TO: The Front Door of 32 Defoe Mansions. Afternoon. *JACK and CATHY arrive at the flat. CATHY's arm is still in a sling, and she looks pale and apprehensive. JACK puts down the empty suitcase he is carrying, and gives her a reassuring smile before ringing the door bell. From inside the flat we hear the chimes.*

JACK: Now leave this to me, Cathy. I'll talk to Doreen, you needn't say anything. Just collect your things.

CATHY nods. JACK presses the button again.

There is a pause.

CATHY: I don't think she's in …

JACK: It doesn't sound like it. (*Quietly to CATHY*) Call her name …

JACK knocks on the door.

CATHY: Doreen!

JACK: (*Shaking his head*) She's not here …

JACK takes PENN's key out of his pocket and unlocks the door.

JACK: Come along, Cathy.

JACK picks up the suitcase and they enter the flat.

CUT TO: The Hall of the Flat.
JACK closes the front door behind him as he and CATHY enter the hall. CATHY moves towards the living room calling "Doreen" as she does so.

139

CATHY: She's out, I'm afraid. (*Indicating the bedroom door on the right*) My things are in here.

JACK opens the bedroom door.

CUT TO: The Bedroom.

JACK and CATHY enter the bedroom. CATHY crosses to a built-in cupboard on the far side of the room. As she slides back the door of the cupboard, JACK puts the empty suitcase down on the bed and opens it. CATHY looks into the cupboard.

CATHY: (*After a moment*) That's funny …

JACK: What is it?

CATHY: My things are here, but Doreen's seem to have disappeared …

JACK: Did she keep all her stuff in here?

CATHY: No, a lot of it's in the other bedroom, but she used to keep her dresses in here because … Wait a minute!

CATHY goes out of the bedroom into the hall. JACK moves across to the cupboard; he is looking at the contents of the cupboard when the telephone rings by the side of the bed. He turns towards the phone and hesitates, undecided whether to answer it or not. Suddenly he makes a decision and picks up the receiver.

JACK: (*On the phone*) Hello? …

OPERATOR: Is that Juniper 1729?

JACK: (*Looking at the dial*) Yes, speaking …

OPERATOR: I have a telegram for Doreen Osborne.

JACK: Thank you, I'll take it.

OPERATOR: It says: "Will expect you ten o'clock tomorrow. Douglas."

JACK: Douglas, did you say?

OPERATOR: Yes, that's right.

JACK: Where was the telegram sent from?

OPERATOR:	It was handed in at St Albans at eleven forty-five …
JACK:	Thank you.
OPERATOR:	Shall I confirm this?
JACK:	Yes – yes, please do.

As JACK thoughtfully replaces the receiver, CATHY returns.

CATHY:	Who was that?

JACK looks up and hesitates.

JACK:	It was a wrong number. Have you discovered anything?
CATHY:	Yes, Doreen's gone – she's left the flat. Her wardrobe's completely empty.
JACK:	(*Nodding*) All right, Cathy, let's get moving. We haven't a lot of time.

CATHY crosses to the open wardrobe and starts collecting her things.

CATHY:	How long will it take us to get to this place?
JACK:	It's about two hours to Bicester – Steeple Aston's about ten miles from there.
CATHY:	Steeple Aston?
JACK:	That's the village, the hotel's called The Priory.
CATHY:	That's an unusual name for an hotel.
JACK:	Yes, I know. It's more a guest house than a hotel – but don't worry, you'll like it all right.
CATHY:	Yes, I'm sure I shall. I shall be glad to get away from London anyway. (*She hesitates, then:*) I'm terribly grateful, Jack, for … what you're doing …
JACK:	There's no need to be grateful, just take care of yourself. And, above all, remember what I've told you. Don't give your address to anyone – don't go out of the hotel – and if you've got to use the telephone, phone me.

CATHY: (*Smiling*) I'll remember that.

JACK: The people who own the hotel are friends of mine,
               and I've told them that you're just recovering from
               a car accident and that you've got to be absolutely
               …

*JACK stops talking, he looks at CATHY. They have obviously
heard something.*

CUT TO: The Front Door of the Flat. Afternoon.
*CLEG REED is letting himself into the flat. He has half a
smoked cigar in his mouth and wears yet another new suit. He
slips the key back into his waistcoat pocket.*

CUT TO: The Hall of the Flat. Afternoon.
*CLEG enters the hall and closes the front door. He looks
towards the living room and then suddenly hesitates, glancing
across at the bedroom door on the right. CATHY has left the
door slightly ajar. CLEG takes a gun out of his pocket and
moves silently towards the bedroom. When he reaches the
bedroom door, he flings out his foot and kicks it wide open. A
frightened CATHY can be seen standing with her back to the
open cupboard, staring across at CLEG.*

CLEG: (*In the doorway*) What the hell are you doing here?
               I thought you were in hospital?

CATHY: I – I came out this morning.

CLEG: Where's Doreen?

CUT TO: The Bedroom. Afternoon.
*JACK is standing flat against the wall, by the open door,
waiting for CLEG to enter the room.*

CATHY: I don't know, Cleg. I think she's left.

CLEG: What do you mean – left?

CATHY: I mean, she's left the flat, gone away …

CLEG steps into the room. He raises the gun and points to the open suitcase on the bed.

CLEG: And what do you think you're up to? What are you planning to do?

As CLEG speaks and raises his arm, JACK springs forward and brings his fist down on the gun. Taken completely by surprise, CLEG half turns in an attempt to identify JACK, then he changes his mind and stoops to pick up the gun. JACK has been waiting for this movement and he quickly brings his hand down, using it as a chopper, on the back of CLEG's neck. As CLEG reels over, JACK picks up the gun – then crosses to the telephone and starts to dial.

CUT TO: The Living Room of JACK KERRY's Flat. Morning.

The telephone is ringing, and JACK comes out of the kitchen wearing a dressing gown over pyjamas and carrying the remains of a glass of milk. He puts the glass down on the table and crosses to the telephone.

JACK: (*On the phone*) Jack Kerry speaking …

CUT TO: A Telephone on a bedside table in a hotel bedroom. Morning.

CATHY is on the telephone.

CATHY: This is Cathy …

CUT TO:

JACK: Hello, Cathy – how are you? Did you sleep well?

CUT TO:

CATHY: Yes, I did; my arm's very much better this morning. I'm not even wearing the sling. Is there any news of Doreen?

CUT TO:

JACK: No; I'm afraid not. I spoke to Superintendent Bromford about twenty minutes ago. They haven't located her, not yet.

CUT TO:

CATHY: Oh dear, I was hoping you'd have found her by now. What about Cleg?

CUT TO:

JACK: They're holding him on a housebreaking charge, but he won't talk; he's playing it very cool at the moment.

The front door bell starts to ring.

CUT TO:

CATHY: I hope Doreen's all right. I'm worried about her.

CUT TO:

JACK: Cathy, there's someone at the door, I'll ring you back later.

CATHY: Yes, all right, Jack.

JACK: Take care of yourself – and remember, don't leave the hotel.

JACK puts the telephone down and goes out into the hall.

CUT TO: The Hall of JACK KERRY's Flat. Day.
LEONARD LINCOLN – dressed for the office, briefcase in hand – is on the verge of ringing the bell again when JACK opens the front door.

JACK: (*Surprised*) Hello, Mr Lincoln!

LEONARD: Good morning. Could you spare me a moment?

JACK: Yes, of course, come along in …

LEONARD: (*Entering the hall*) I say, I hope I haven't got you out of bed?

JACK: No, I've been up for some time; I just haven't got round to getting dressed yet.

CUT TO: The Living Room of JACK KERRY's Flat. Day.

JACK enters the living room followed by LEONARD.

JACK: Can I offer you anything?

LEONARD: No, thank you. Kerry, I've been going through my aunt's things, and yesterday I had to make a decision about the dog – Midge. In the end I decided to take it down to a friend of mine who lives in the country.

JACK: Where was the dog, at the hotel?

LEONARD: Yes, curiously enough they rather encourage pets, that's probably why my aunt picked the hotel in the first place. Incidentally, you know it was all nonsense about her working there? She was actually staying at the hotel.

JACK: (*Interrupting LEONARD*) Yes, I know, but what is it you want to tell me about the dog?

LEONARD: Well, when I picked up Midge, the first thing I noticed was his collar. It was obviously brand new and in view of the fuss my aunt made about the original one – the one your father gave her – I thought I'd take a jolly good look at this one.

LEONARD opens his briefcase and takes out a brand-new dog collar.

LEONARD: Here it is …

JACK: (*Taking the collar*) Is there anything unusual about it?

LEONARD: Yes …

JACK looks at the collar: on turning it over he discovers a zip fastener, running almost the length of the collar itself. He glances at LEONARD, then pulls back the zip and examines the concealed pocket.

JACK: Was there anything in this pocket?

LEONARD: Yes, there was.

LEONARD takes a piece of paper out of his waistcoat.

LEONARD: Something belonging to you, Kerry.

JACK: (*Curious*) Belonging to me?

JACK takes the slip of paper from LEONARD.

JACK: What is it?

LEONARD: It appears to be a receipt; for a pearl necklace.

JACK looks at LEONARD, then at the slip of paper in his hand. We see the receipt. The printed heading reads:

"Minerva Jewels, Ltd., Burlington Arcade, London, W.1."

There is a reference number, 14961, on the paper and the hastily scribbled words: "Kerry – Triple row graduated pearls, restrung".

JACK: (*Looking at LEONARD*) This isn't mine; but I can understand why you thought it was.

LEONARD: But it's made out to you, it's got your name on it.

JACK: No, it's made out to my father. But I know all about it, Lincoln – thank you very much for bringing it to me.

LEONARD: You know all about it?

JACK: Yes.

LEONARD: Do you mean – you know my aunt had it? You knew it was in the collar?

JACK: No; but I knew the receipt existed. As a matter of fact, we've been looking for it.

LEONARD: (*Puzzled*) I see. (*Suddenly*) No, I'm damned if I see! If the receipt belonged to your father what was my aunt doing with it? And why hide it in a dog collar, for Pete's sake? And there's another thing, Kerry! This collar's been especially made,

146

JACK: you can't just walk into a shop and buy one like this, I'm jolly sure of that.

JACK: (*His thoughts elsewhere*) No; no, you can't. You're right, Lincoln. I'd like to keep the collar and receipt, if I may?

LEONARD: Yes, of course, by all means. (*Hesitantly*) Kerry, I spoke to Superintendent Bromford yesterday. I asked him if there was any news, any chance of an arrest, and he said there wasn't. But I had the feeling that – well, that he was concealing something.

JACK: Well, if he is, he's concealing it from me as well. Lincoln, will you excuse me – I've got an appointment at half past nine and, as you see, I'm not even dressed yet.

LEONARD: Yes, of course.

JACK and LEONARD cross towards the hall.

CUT TO: The Box Room. JACK KERRY's Flat. Morning.
DOUGLAS comes up the spiral staircase from the office; he carries a folder and several letters. He knocks on the door and enters the living room.

CUT TO: The Living Room of JACK KERRY's Flat. Morning.
DOUGLAS enters the room; he hears voices and looks towards the hall. As he does so, he notices the dog collar which JACK has left on the table.

CUT TO: The Hall of JACK KERRY's Flat. Morning.
JACK is closing the front door on LEONARD LINCOLN. He turns, and thoughtfully moves back towards the living room. He is still holding the jeweller's receipt in his hand.

CUT TO: The Living Room of JACK KERRY's Flat.
Morning.

DOUGLAS has now picked up the collar and is examining the
zip fastener when JACK re-enters from the hall.

DOUGLAS: Jack, what on earth is this? Where did it come
from?

JACK briskly crosses to the telephone.

JACK: I'll tell you all about that in a minute, Doug. I
want to use the phone.

DOUGLAS: Is it private, because if it is …

JACK: No, no … (*With the suggestion of a smile*) It
certainly isn't private so far as you're
concerned.

JACK looks at the phone as he dials.

JACK: (*Casually*) Douglas – do you know a girl called
Doreen Osborne?

DOUGLAS: (*Looking up*) Doreen …?

JACK: Osborne …

DOUGLAS: No, I don't …

JACK: Have you heard of her?

DOUGLAS: No, I'm afraid I haven't. Should I have done?

JACK: (*On the phone, turns from DOUGLAS;*
suddenly) Hello? … I want to send a telegram
…

OPERATOR: (*On the other end*) Could I have the
subscriber's number, please?

JACK: Juniper 1874 …

OPERATOR: Thank you. Where are you sending it to, sir?

JACK: It's to Mrs Iris Bannister … Stillwater,
Lawrence Avenue, Hampstead … London,
N.W.3.

On hearing the name Bannister, DOUGLAS looks at JACK
obviously curious.

OPERATOR: Go ahead …

JACK: Have found receipt … Suggest we meet Danish Café, Hampstead … Four o'clock this afternoon …

OPERATOR: Danish Café, Hampstead … Four o'clock this afternoon …

JACK: That's right. The name of the sender is Croft. Douglas Croft.

DOUGLAS puts the collar down on the table and stares at JACK in amazement.

CUT TO: The Danish Café, Hampstead, London. Afternoon. This is a small brightly lit café with most of the tables in alcoves.

JACK is sitting in one of the alcoves drinking a cup of tea. GRETA, a good-looking girl of about twenty-five is busy behind the bar counter. CHARLES BANNISTER enters from the street and crosses towards the counter. He wears dark flannel trousers and a flower in the buttonhole of his single-breasted blazer. He has seen JACK and as he reaches the counter, he turns and looks quickly at him.

BANNISTER: (*To GRETA*) Good afternoon to you, Greta … Twenty cigarettes, my dear … The usual kind …

GRETA gives BANNISTER a packet of cigarettes and he puts the money on the counter.

BANNISTER: And bring me a cup of tea … with a slice of lemon … I'm joining the gentleman over there.

GRETA: Yes, Mr Bannister.

BANNISTER leaves the counter and crosses down to JACK. He stands by the table opening the packet of cigarettes.

BANNISTER: My wife sends you her apologies. She's got rather a busy afternoon, she just couldn't make it.

149

JACK: Not to worry. To tell the truth, it was you I was
               expecting, Mr Bannister. (*He glances at his
               watch*) But you're a little late, I'm afraid. Did
               you have trouble parking the wheelchair?

*BANNISTER smiles and sits down facing JACK, putting the
open packet of cigarettes on the table.*

BANNISTER: Your telegram, Mr Kerry – was it fact or
               fiction?

JACK: I'm not sure I understand you. I have the
               receipt for the necklace, if that's what you
               mean?

BANNISTER: That's what I mean. Could I see it?

*JACK hesitates, then takes the receipt out of his pocket and
shows it to BANNISTER who stares at the slip of paper but
makes no attempt to take it.*

BANNISTER: Thank you. (*He lights his cigarette and looks
               at JACK for a moment*) When did you first hear
               about this receipt?

JACK: (*Looking at the receipt*) Your wife got in touch
               with a friend of mine.

BANNISTER: (*Nodding*) Douglas Croft … He used to work
               for your father …

JACK: (*Looking up*) That's right. Mrs Bannister
               telephoned Douglas. She said she thought my
               father had put the receipt somewhere and …

BANNISTER: She asked Croft to look for it?

JACK: Yes.

BANNISTER: And he found it?

JACK: No – someone else found it.

BANNISTER: I see. But I still don't get the point of the
               telegram. Couldn't you have posted the receipt
               to my wife?

JACK: Yes, but in that case, I would have been spared
               the pleasure of your company, Mr Bannister.
               (*Smiling*) And that wasn't what I had in mind.
BANNISTER: (*Quietly*) What had you in mind? What is it
               you want?
JACK: (*Leaning towards BANNISTER*) I want to
               know how my father got involved in this affair
               – I want to know why Mel Harris murdered
               him?
BANNISTER: Your father was a fool – and an unlucky one at
               that. My advice to you, young man, is don't get
               mixed up in this business.
JACK: And supposing I don't take your advice?
BANNISTER: I can't imagine you'd be that stupid.
JACK: Can't you? Supposing I am that stupid, Mr
               Bannister?
BANNISTER: Well, in that case ... You saw what happened
               to Doreen Osborne.
JACK: Yes – but I don't scare that easily. I've seen
               people beaten up before.
BANNISTER: I'm sure you have – but it's not you I'm
               thinking of.
JACK: No? Then who are you thinking of? (*A
               moment; angry*) Who are you thinking of –
               Cathy White?
BANNISTER: (*Nodding*) I'm quite sure you wouldn't like
               anything unfortunate to happen to Miss White.
JACK: You're dead right, I wouldn't. And nothing is
               going to happen to her!
BANNISTER: You sound very confident.
JACK: I'm confident – all right!
BANNISTER: Why? Because you don't think we could find
               her? (*Smiling*) Would you like me to tell you

where Miss White is, at this precise moment, Mr Kerry?

JACK: Yes, I would. Go ahead ...

BANNISTER: She's staying at a hotel called The Priory, it's at Steeple Aston, a small village about ten miles from Bicester.

JACK looks at BANNISTER for a moment, his expression serious – then suddenly his expression changes and he leans forward and helps himself to one of BANNISTER's cigarettes.

JACK: (*Smiling; curiously confident*) You wouldn't like to bet on that, would you, Mr Bannister?

JACK is still smiling as he flicks his lighter and holds it up to the cigarette.

END OF EPISODE FIVE

EPISODE SIX

OPEN TO: The Danish Café, Hampstead, London.
Afternoon.

CHARLES BANNISTER is sitting at the table in the alcove, facing JACK.

BANNISTER: … Would you like me to tell you where Miss White is, at this precise moment, Mr Kerry?

JACK: Yes, I would. Go ahead …

BANNISTER: She's staying at a hotel called The Priory, it's at Steeple Aston, a small village about ten miles from Bicester.

JACK looks at BANNISTER for a moment, his expression serious – then suddenly his expression changes and he leans forward and helps himself to one of BANNISTER's cigarettes.

JACK: (*Smiling; curiously confident*) You wouldn't like to bet on that, would you, Mr Bannister?

JACK lights his cigarette.

BANNISTER: (*Quietly; puzzled*) What do you mean – I wouldn't like to bet on it?

JACK: Yesterday afternoon, I picked up Cathy and took her to Doreen Osborne's – we collected her things. While we were there, Cleg Reed showed up. I'm sure I don't have to tell you what happened to Mr Reed.

BANNISTER: Go on …

JACK: After I'd dealt with Reed, I searched the bedroom. I found the hidden 'mike' and the tape recorder. I knew it had already recorded my conversation with Cathy about the hotel at Steeple Aston, so I left the contraption there – in the flat, just as it was. (*Smiling*) I'm afraid it provided you with what your American friends call a 'bum steer', Mr Bannister.

BANNISTER: (*A shade angry*) It didn't provide me with anything. I told Mel Harris a long time ago that

155

> he'd be making a mistake if he under-rated you
> …

BANNISTER stops talking, his eyes now on GRETA, the waitress, who is standing by the table.

GRETA: Excuse me, Mr Bannister – you're wanted on the phone.

BANNISTER: (*Surprised*) I am? You're sure it's for me?

GRETA: Yes – the lady asked for you, sir.

BANNISTER: Where is the phone?

GRETA points to a curtained recess at the end of the room.

GRETA: It's over there, sir, through that curtain.

BANNISTER nods to GRETA, looks at JACK, then rises from the table and crosses down to the recess. He draws back the curtain. There is a wall telephone, with the receiver hanging from the hook.

CUT TO: A Telephone Box, Hampstead, London. Afternoon.

IRIS BANNISTER is in the box, waiting for her husband; she looks agitated and faintly worried. She speaks the moment BANNISTER takes the receiver.

IRIS: Hello? Charles?

CUT TO:

BANNISTER: (*On the phone*) Iris, what is it?

CUT TO:

IRIS: Charles, I think there's going to be trouble …

BANNISTER: Trouble? What kind of trouble?

IRIS: Mel's here – he's watching the café!

CUT TO:

BANNISTER: (*Surprised*) Are you sure?

156

CUT TO:

IRIS: Yes, he's driven round the block twice already
              …

BANNISTER: Are you sure it's Mel?

IRIS: Yes, I'm positive. He's in the grey Jaguar.
              (*Tensely*) Someone must have tipped him off –
              what are we going to do?

CUT TO:

BANNISTER: Has he seen you?

CUT TO:

IRIS: No, I don't think so. But he's probably seen the
              car. I had to leave it in Heath Street.

CUT TO:

BANNISTER: Where are you now, Iris – where are you
              speaking from?

CUT TO:

IRIS: I'm in the box near the café, opposite the
              chemist's.

CUT TO:

BANNISTER: (*Looking worried, undecided what to do*) All
              right – don't worry, I'll bluff it out. Leave the
              car where it is and go home. I'll see you later.

CUT TO:

IRIS: But what are you going to do? Mel knows
              you've been talking to Kerry, so he's …

CUT TO:

BANNISTER: Do as I say, Iris! I'll join you later. There's probably nothing to worry about anyway... (*He replaces the receiver*)

CUT TO: The Café. Afternoon.

JACK is sitting at the table watching the recess. GRETA comes across to the table with a cup of tea as BANNISTER appears and returns to the table.

BANNISTER: Kerry, we'll have to continue our conversation some other time. I'll phone you tomorrow morning.

BANNISTER takes a half-crown out of his pocket and puts it on the table.

BANNISTER: Sorry about the tea, Greta. Keep the change.

GRETA, a shade surprised, picks up the half-crown. JACK watches BANNISTER as he leaves the café.

JACK: (*To GRETA*) How much do I owe you?

GRETA: One-and-six, please, sir.

JACK: (*Sorting out his change*) I gather it was a lady on the phone.

GRETA: Yes; seems to have had his marching orders, doesn't he? (*Scribbling on her pad*) Sounded like Mrs Bannister to me. Whoever it was, she was in quite a tizz.

JACK: (*Offering money*) Do the Bannisters often come in here?

GRETA: Thank you, sir. They used to do, quite a lot at one time. For coffee mostly. We haven't seen so much of them just recently.

GRETA picks up the cup of tea and returns to the counter. JACK sits for a moment, deep in thought – then he rises from the table. As he does so a car can be heard outside – racing past the café. Suddenly, a woman screams, and this is followed almost immediately by the sound of angry voices. As the roar of the car fades away, we hear the usual accumulation of noises associated with a street accident. In the café, people turn instinctively towards the door. JACK quickly leaves the table, grabbing his hat and coat as he moves towards the street.

CUT TO: A Street in Hampstead, London. Afternoon.
People are running along the street towards the hit-and-run victim. In the distance, we can see the lifeless body of CHARLES BANNISTER lying in the road. JACK comes out of the café and quickly takes in the situation. He joins the people racing towards the scene of the accident.

A group of people are gathered around the body of CHARLES BANNISTER. A young man is making a brief examination of the dead man. JACK stands watching him, aware of the excited and angry comments of the onlookers.

ONLOOKERS' COMMENTS:

1: It was deliberate! It must have been!
2: My God, I've never seen anything like it! Never! I was just going to cross the road when this car …
3: It was a Jag! A bloody, whacking big Jag!
4: I didn't see him … It happened so quickly … I was looking at the chap in the road and then … I just couldn't believe it … I just couldn't believe it!
5: Yes, 'course it was a Jag!

Suddenly, IRIS BANNISTER arrives and pushes her way through the crowd. As she does so, the young man rises and, looking at JACK, slowly shakes his head. IRIS turns towards JACK; she is still breathless … frightened … After a moment, she forces herself to look down at the body of her husband. JACK moves towards her, gently taking hold of her arm.

CUT TO: The Living Room of JACK KERRY's Flat. Evening.

JACK is mixing a whisky and soda. He crosses and gives the drink to HAL BROMFORD. The SUPERINTENDENT is sitting in an armchair, nibbling at his pipe, as he watches JACK.

JACK: I hope that's to your liking, sir.

BROMFORD: It looks highly satisfactory. (*Taking the drink*) Thank you, Kerry.

JACK returns to the table and picks up a tankard of beer which has already been poured, he turns and crosses to the settee.

JACK: It was very good of you to come here, sir – especially at a moment's notice. I appreciate it.

BROMFORD: Why did you send for me?

JACK: I wanted to have a talk with you, but I thought if I came to the office there was a chance that … (*He looks at BROMFORD*) I've found out the truth, sir – about my father …

BROMFORD: (*Interested*) Go on, Kerry …

JACK: This afternoon, after Charles Bannister was killed, I took his wife – Iris – back to the house. She was in a terrible state. I let her talk, I thought if only she … (*A shrug*) I couldn't have stopped her anyway, even if I'd wanted to. She told me about my father and Mrs Lincoln. She explained why Rupert Delaney …

BROMFORD: (*Interrupting JACK*) Kerry, I'd like to hear what Mrs Bannister told you, but don't you think you'd better start at the beginning?

JACK: (*With a nod*) Yes, I'm sorry. Apparently, before Mrs Lincoln worked for my father, she had a variety of jobs and rather a chequered career, I'm afraid. One day she discovered that a man she used to work for – a man known as

	Mel Harris – was running a call-girl racket. She collected evidence of his activities – photographs, lists of agents, a photostat of an incriminating letter he'd written, etc – and she started blackmailing him. Suddenly, she realised the risk she was taking, and she told Harris that if anything should happen to her, Bob Kerry, my father, would take over. In short: she inferred that she and my father were working together …
BROMFORD:	Which wasn't true …?
JACK:	No, of course it wasn't – and even Mel Harris had his doubts about it. He told Iris Bannister to get friendly with my father and report back to him. Iris reported that, in her opinion, Mrs Lincoln had lied; she also reported the fact that Mrs Lincoln was absolutely crazy about her dog, Midge. You can guess what happened.
BROMFORD:	They kidnapped the dog and offered to return it in exchange for the letters and the photostats …
JACK:	Right. Delaney – on behalf of Mel Harris, of course – telephoned Mrs Lincoln and they arranged to meet. That's when Mrs Lincoln, incidentally, not my father, made a note of the car number. She met Rupert and he drove her back to his flat and showed her the dog collar – to prove that they had, in fact, got the poodle. But Mrs Lincoln wouldn't play, and Mel Harris decided there was only one thing to do …
BROMFORD:	… Scare the hell out of her by killing your father.

JACK: Yes. Harris and Cleg Reed followed my father to the golf club. They waylaid him. Cleg knocked him unconscious, then Harris took a heavy stone and … Afterwards, they put the stone in the bunker together with …

BROMFORD: … your father's body.

JACK: Yes. Rupert Delaney, who was already on the course, then came forward with his prepared story about the golf ball hitting my father …

BROMFORD: And your father falling and striking his head on the stone …

JACK: Right.

BROMFORD: Well, I must confess it ties in with what Cathy White told you. But I don't quite see why Delaney sent you that note – and the collar?

JACK: Delaney didn't send it.

BROMFORD: Then who did?

JACK: Cathy … You see by this time Cathy had an inkling of what was going on. She felt confident that the best thing for Rupert was for him to see me and make a clean breast of things. But she knew he never would – not unless something, or someone, forced him into it. Then suddenly, she hit on the idea of sending me the dog collar and the note. That night she told Rupert what she'd done, and she gave him the receipt. She told him that the very next day he'd be interrogated by the police and, if he had any guts, he'd tell them the whole story. Unfortunately, they had a row – Rupert went back to his flat and sent for Mel Harris. (*A shrug*) I don't have to tell you how Mr Harris solved the problem.

BROMFORD: No, you don't. (*He rises*) But there's one thing you can tell me, Kerry.

KERRY: What's that, sir?

There is a pause.

BROMFORD: (*Looking at JACK*) Who is Mel Harris?

CUT TO: The Living Room of JACK KERRY's flat. Morning.

The telephone is ringing. JACK comes out of the kitchen carrying a glass of milk. He is wearing grey flannel trousers: his jacket is on the arm of the settee.

JACK: (*On the phone*) Juniper 1874 …

CUT TO: ED ROYCE's Office at Scotland Yard.

ED is on the telephone in his office.

ED: Is that you, Jack?

CUT TO:

JACK: Hello, Ed!

CUT TO:

ED: I've got some news for you. We've found Doreen Osborne …

CUT TO:

JACK: Where is she?

CUT TO:

ED: Your hunch was right. She's in a nursing home at St Albans. She's having an operation on her face the day after tomorrow.

CUT TO:

JACK: Have you seen her?

163

CUT TO:

ED: No, but Sergeant Quilter has. I'm afraid she won't talk, Jack – she won't say anything.

CUT TO:

JACK: Where is this nursing home?

CUT TO:

ED: It's in Maylee Park, St Albans. It's run by a plastic surgeon called Douglas – Doctor Walter Douglas. Very clever chap according to all accounts.

CUT TO:

JACK: (*Thoughtfully*) All right, Ed. Thank you for phoning.

JACK replaces the phone and stands for a moment deep in thought. There is a knock on the box room door and DOUGLAS CROFT appears. He carries a morning newspaper.

DOUGLAS: May I come in?

JACK: Yes, of course, Doug.

DOUGLAS: Jack, I've just been reading about this man Bannister and the car accident. Was he the man who …

JACK: (*Interrupting DOUGLAS*) It wasn't an accident. Bannister was murdered – he was run down.

DOUGLAS: You mean – deliberately?

JACK: (*Looking at DOUGLAS*) Yes …

DOUGLAS: (*Incredulously*) Are you sure?

JACK: Yes. I'm quite sure.

DOUGLAS: Were you there when it happened? Did you see the car?

JACK: No, I didn't. I was in the café. I'd been talking to Bannister. He'd only just left me.

164

DOUGLAS: (*Curious*) Bannister had?

JACK: Yes. You remember the telegram I sent? Well, Charles Bannister turned up instead of his wife. (*Glancing at his watch*) Look, Doug – will you excuse me?

JACK crosses to the settee and picks up his jacket.

JACK: I'd like to tell you about this, but I've got someone coming to see me …

DOUGLAS: (*Puzzled by JACK's manner*) Yes, of course. It's none of my business anyway …

JACK: (*Friendly*) No, no, I didn't mean that! As a matter of fact, I was going to have a talk with you this morning. I may need your help.

The door bell starts to ring.

DOUGLAS: (*Puzzled*) My help?

JACK: Yes. (*He glances towards the hall*) But I'll talk to you about this later, Douglas. You'll be in the shop all morning?

DOUGLAS: Yes, of course. I've got an appointment with Allied Sports at three o'clock, but that's all.

DOUGLAS crosses to the box room.

JACK: I'll see you before then.

DOUGLAS glances across at the hall, still puzzled by JACK's manner.

DOUGLAS: Yes, all right, Jack.

DOUGLAS nods to JACK and goes into the box room. JACK looks towards the hall, then moves to the box room door and, opening it, quickly glances into the room. Apparently satisfied that DOUGLAS has returned to the office via the spiral staircase he closes the door, turns the key in the lock, and crosses over into the hall.

CUT TO: The Front Door of the Flat. Morning.

CATHY WHITE, accompanied by a uniformed police driver – SERGEANT FULLER – is standing at the front door, her finger on the bell. FULLER is a cheerful looking man in his late thirties.

CATHY: It's all right, Sergeant – you can go now.

FULLER smiles and shakes his head.

FULLER: My orders were to deliver you personally, Miss.

The door opens.

JACK: Hello, Cathy! Come along in!

FULLER: Good morning, sir.

JACK: Thank you, Sergeant! Thank you very much …

FULLER: (*Grinning*) It's a pleasure. (*To CATHY*) Any time, Miss … Just ask the Inspector to give us a buzz. We can be very useful in the rush hour.

CATHY smiles.

CUT TO: The Living Room of the flat. Morning.

CATHY enters from the hall, followed by JACK.

JACK: Have you had breakfast?

CATHY: Yes, I'd just finished when the Sergeant arrived.

JACK: (*Smiling*) Were you surprised when I phoned you?

CATHY: Well – yes, I was.

JACK: (*Indicating the settee*) Sit down, Cathy. Would you like a cup of coffee?

CATHY: No, thank you – but I'd like a cigarette, if you've got one …

CATHY sits on the settee.

JACK: Yes, of course.

JACK takes a box of cigarettes from the table and offers CATHY one. CATHY's hand is shaking slightly as she takes the cigarette. JACK watches her as he flicks his lighter and holds it out to her.

JACK: You look worried.

CATHY: I'm afraid I am.

JACK: Why? Because of what happened yesterday?

CATHY: Yes. It wasn't an accident – Charles Bannister was murdered.

JACK: I know that. I know why he was murdered, too.

JACK sits down beside CATHY.

JACK: Cathy, I saw Superintendent Bromford this morning; we had a long talk and … We want you to help us.

CATHY: I'll do anything I can, I've already told you that.

JACK: Yes, I know, but – I want you to realise what you're doing; what you're letting yourself in for.

CATHY: (*Puzzled*) What is it you want me to do?

JACK: Well, first of all, we want you to talk to Doreen Osborne.

CATHY: But I don't know where Doreen is, I haven't seen her since …

JACK: She's in a nursing home at St Albans. She's having an operation on her face the day after tomorrow. We'd like you to see her before the operation.

CATHY: All right, but … (*She shakes her head*) If I know Doreen, she'll be too frightened to talk. She won't say anything, not now, it's too late.

JACK: I realise that.

CATHY: Then why do you want me to see her? What's the point?

There is a pause.

JACK: (*Looking at CATHY*) We want you to do the talking, Cathy – not Doreen Osborne.

CUT TO: A Private Room in a Nursing Home, St Albans. Morning.

DOREEN OSBORNE is sitting up in bed looking towards CATHY, who is standing with her back to the room, staring out

167

of a large bay window. There is a table with a telephone, some books and an ashtray. DOREEN's Siamese cat is in a basket on the floor, near the window.

DOREEN: I'm damned if I understand you, Cathy! I don't know what you're talking about – I just don't know what you're getting at!

CATHY turns from the window and crossing to the table, flicks the ash off the cigarette she is smoking into the ashtray. Her manner appears to be different – she is brisk, almost unfriendly. It is obvious that DOREEN is puzzled by her.

CATHY: I'm not getting at anything, Doreen. I'm simply asking you to deliver a message for me.

DOREEN doesn't look at CATHY.

DOREEN: How can I deliver a message to someone I don't even know?

CATHY: Oh, for God's sake, don't treat me like a child! You know Mel Harris – you've had dealings with him. You've spoken to him on the phone – not once, but hundreds of times.

DOREEN: (*Tensely*) Cathy, why do you think I'm in here? Why do you think I'm going to have this bloody operation tomorrow? I was beaten up, and I was beaten up because Mel Harris thought ...

CATHY: (*Interrupting DOREEN*) Doreen, all I'm asking you to do is deliver a message! If I knew Harris – if I knew how to contact him, I'd do it myself.

DOREEN: (*After a moment*) What ... is this message?

CATHY: Tell him I've been in to see you – tell him I've returned to your flat and I want to talk to him. Ask him to see me tomorrow morning at eleven o'clock.

DOREEN: (*Shaking her head*) He won't see you. He'll send Cleg Reed, and you know what that little bastard ...

CATHY: He can't send Reed – the police have picked him up.

DOREEN: (*Astonished*) Cleg?

CATHY: Yes; they're holding him on a murder charge.

DOREEN: (*Delighted*) When did this happen?

CATHY ignores this question.

CATHY: Doreen, I haven't a lot of time. I've got to be back in Town by one o'clock. Will you do this for me – or won't you?

DOREEN looks at CATHY for a moment.

DOREEN: Supposing I do – supposing I phone Mel Harris and he asks me why you want to see him. What do I say?

CATHY: You tell him the truth. You tell him you don't know why I want to see him.

DOREEN: He'll want a reason; he's not going to accept …

CATHY: All right! Tell him I want Rupert's job. The same flat – the same terms – the same set-up …

DOREEN: (*Stunned*) You mean, you want to work for Harris? … You want … you're not serious?

CATHY: I'm deadly serious! I'm sick to hell of playing around, Doreen. I know what Rupert was making, I know how he operated – there's no reason on earth why I shouldn't take over and do precisely the same.

DOREEN: But only the other day you told me that you didn't know about Rupert! You said you thought he was running a property racket and …

CATHY: (*Interrupting DOREEN, looking at her watch*) Look, Doreen – I've got to have an answer. Will you ring Mel Harris for me, or won't you?

DOREEN pauses for a moment.

DOREEN: Yes, I'll ring him. But you're making a terrible mistake, Cathy. If you take my advice …

169

CATHY: (*Almost losing her temper*) I don't want your advice, Doreen – I just want you to do what I'm asking you to do!

DOREEN: All right, I'll phone him tonight. (*She shakes her head*) But he won't play. He won't see you.

CATHY: I think he will.

DOREEN: You don't know Mel Harris.

CATHY: No – and he doesn't know me. Tell him I was a friend of Mrs Lincoln's. A very close friend.

CATHY stubs out her cigarette in the ashtray.

CATHY: Tell him we used to have long, cosy little chats together.

CUT TO: Outside the Front Entrance of Defoe Mansions. Morning.

A taxi pulls up about fifty yards short of the block of flats. ED ROYCE gets out of it. He wears a light-coloured suit and appears to be in no particular hurry. He gives a friendly nod to the driver as he pays him. Then he strolls casually along the pavement. Not once does he glance in the direction of Defoe Mansions. The camera slowly pans ED as he walks past the entrance to Defoe Mansions and telephone box on the corner of the road.

CUT TO: Inside the Telephone Box near Defoe Mansions. Morning.

DOUGLAS CROFT is in the telephone box, watching ED as he strolls along the pavement. DOUGLAS is holding the receiver, but he doesn't appear to be in conversation with anyone – his eyes are on ED ROYCE and the entrance to the block of flats.

CUT TO: Defoe Mansions. The Tradesman's Entrance at the rear of the building. Morning.

A small van is parked near the tradesman's entrance, and to the right of a fire escape – which extends from the basement of the building to the roof. ED ROYCE appears in the distance, apparently strolling towards the tradesman's entrance – or the fire escape. About ten or twenty yards from the fire escape he stops and takes a packet of cigarettes out of his pocket. As he lights his cigarette he glances with obvious interest at the van.

CUT TO: The Living Room of 32 Defoe Mansions – DOREEN OSBORNE's Flat. Morning.

The telephone is ringing. CATHY comes out of the main bedroom, closing the door behind her, and crosses to the phone: as she reaches the table the phone stops ringing. CATHY hesitates, is about to pick up the receiver, then turns and looks towards the hall. The front door chimes can be heard.

CUT TO: The Hall of the Flat. Morning.

CATHY arrives from the living room and, crossing the hall, opens the front door. She finds herself face to face with NORMAN PENN. He is apparently surprised to see her.

PENN: Oh … Good morning …

CATHY: Good morning.

PENN: Can I have a word with Miss Osborne, please?

CATHY: (*Looking at PENN; curious*) I'm afraid she's not here at the moment.

PENN: Oh – oh dear! How very unfortunate.

CATHY: Can I help you? I'm a friend of Miss Osborne's.

PENN: Well – my name is Penn, Norman Penn. I have a pet shop in St John's Wood, and Doreen – er – Miss Osborne …

CATHY: Oh, yes, of course! I've heard Doreen speak of you! Do come in, Mr Penn …

PENN: (*Hesitating*) Er … (*Entering the hall*) Thank you.

The front door remains partly open during CATHY's conversation with PENN in the hall.

CATHY: Doreen's away – she's had an operation; I doubt whether she'll be home until the end of the week.

PENN: Oh, I didn't realise that, I thought … Well, it's not important …

CATHY: Are you sure I can't help you?

PENN: No … it's very kind of you, but … Well, it's just that Miss Osborne said she might be interested in buying another Siamese cat and I've seen one … She has one already, you know.

CATHY: Yes, I know … Chow …

PENN is seemingly delighted that CATHY knows what he is talking about.

PENN: That's right … Chow … A sweet little thing … Yesterday a customer of mine brought me another one – just like Chow … An absolute darling … Perfect pedigree … I feel sure she'd sell it if the price was right …

CATHY: Why don't you phone Doreen and have a word with her about it? In any case, I'm sure she'd be pleased to hear from you. She's in the Maylee Park Nursing Home, St Albans. I'm afraid I haven't got the number, but it's bound to be in the book.

PENN: Thank you. That's a very good idea – I'll do that.

PENN hesitates, then opens the door.

PENN: It's really very kind of you. Goodbye, Miss–?

CATHY: Goodbye, Mr Penn.

CATHY smiles at PENN then closes the door. She stands with her back to it, obviously puzzled and a shade tense. Suddenly, the telephone starts ringing again in the living room.

CUT TO: The Living Room.
CATHY quickly enters the room and picks up the phone.
CATHY: Hello? Who is that?

CUT TO: The Telephone Box near Defoe Mansions. Morning.
DOUGLAS is on the phone; he looks tense and sounds a shade excited.
DOUGLAS: Miss White?
CATHY: Yes, speaking …
DOUGLAS: This is Douglas Croft. He's arrived – I've seen
            him! He's in the building …

CUT TO: The Living Room. Morning.
CATHY: (*On the phone*) Thank you …
CATHY replaces the receiver and slowly turns towards the hall. As she goes so the front door chimes can be heard again. CATHY goes out into the hall.

CUT TO: The Hall of the Flat. Morning.
CATHY enters the hall and crosses to the front door. She hesitates, as if undecided whether to open the door or not, then suddenly makes up her mind and opens it. NORMAN PENN is standing in the doorway.
PENN: (*A shade embarrassed*) I'm terribly sorry to
            trouble you again, but – did you say the nursing
            home was called Merton?
CATHY: No – Maylee … M.A.Y.L. Double E …
PENN: (*With a little laugh*) Yes, of course … How
            very stupid of me! … Maylee … Now
            whatever made me think of Merton?
CATHY: Maylee Park Nursing Home, St Albans …
PENN: I've got it now. (*Shaking his head*) I'm not terribly
            bright this morning, I'm afraid.

173

CATHY opens the door wider.

CATHY: If you'd like to come in, Mr Penn, I'll write the address down for you.

PENN looks at CATHY; he appears to be on the verge of accepting her invitation, then suddenly changes his mind.

PENN: No … No, it's all right, I can remember it now, I'm quite sure. (*Touching his hat*) Thank you again – you've been most helpful.

PENN turns and goes. CATHY stands holding the door looking out into the corridor. After a moment, she closes the door and turns towards the living room.

CUT TO: The Living Room of the Flat.

CATHY enters the living room and stops dead – her eyes on the bedroom. The bedroom door is now wide open. The camera slowly pans from the open bedroom door to the cocktail bar in the corner of the room. ED ROYCE is sitting on a stool, his back to the tall counter, looking at CATHY.

There is a pause.

CATHY: (*Quietly*) How did you get in?

ED: (*Indicating the bedroom door*) From the fire escape – through the bedroom. (*A moment*) You look frightened.

CATHY: I am. I'm scared to hell.

The front door chimes can be heard.

ED: Don't worry, it'll be all right. (*With a smile*) Everything's under control.

CATHY turns towards the hall, then looks at ED again.

ED: Here he is … (*He climbs down from the bar*) Now don't forget, play it cool – and for God's sake watch his hands …

ED gives CATHY a reassuring pat on the arm as he crosses towards the bedroom.

CUT TO: The Hall of the Flat.

CATHY enters the hall and after a momentary hesitation – a nervous intake of breath – she opens the front door. LEONARD LINCOLN is standing in the doorway. He wears a dark suit and carries a homburg hat and a briefcase.

LEONARD: (*Pleasantly*) Miss White?

CATHY: Yes?

LEONARD: Good morning! My name is Lincoln. Leonard Lincoln, Storm Insurance Company. I think we have an appointment, Miss White …

CATHY: An appointment?

LEONARD: Yes – it was made yesterday through a mutual friend – Doreen Osborne. (*Smiling*) Unless of course I'm mistaken?

CATHY looks at LEONARD, unsmiling.

CATHY: (*Apparently very sure of herself*) No, you're not mistaken. I've been expecting you. Come along in …

CATHY opens the door wider.

CUT TO: The Living Room of the Flat.

LEONARD LINCOLN enters followed by CATHY. He puts his hat and valise down on the settee and stands for a moment taking stock of his surroundings.

CATHY: What did you say your name was?

LEONARD: (*Not looking at CATHY*) I said Lincoln – but you can call me Harris, or Mel, or Mr Harris, whichever you prefer, Miss White.

CATHY: What do your friends call you? Assuming of course, you have friends?

LEONARD: (*Looking at CATHY and smiling*) Oh, I have friends. Some very influential ones. You'd be surprised.

175

LEONARD strolls around the room and looks at the bedroom door.

LEONARD: However, I didn't come here to discuss my friends.

LEONARD stops near the bedroom door.

LEONARD: I understand you want something from me?

CATHY: Yes.

LEONARD: What?

CATHY: I want a job. The one Rupert had.

LEONARD: Are you sure that's what you want?

CATHY: Yes – I want his job; and his flat.

LEONARD: (*After a moment*) But you saw what happened to Rupert.

CATHY: Yes.

LEONARD: Doesn't that frighten you?

CATHY: Yes, it frightens me; but Rupert was stupid – he lost his nerve. I don't lose my nerve quite so easily.

LEONARD: (*Looking at CATHY*) No, I don't think you do.

LEONARD looks down at the key in the bedroom door and casually, almost without realising what he is doing, turns it in the lock. CATHY is apparently unaware of this movement.

CATHY: Well – what do you say?

LEONARD: (*Turning*) Say?

CATHY: About the job – and the flat?

LEONARD: I'd like to think about it. (*He crosses to the hall*) I'd like to know just a little more about you before I make a decision.

CATHY: But you know quite a lot about me.

LEONARD: Not enough.

LEONARD suddenly closes the door leading into the hall shutting off the hallway from the living room. There is now no escape from the room and CATHY realises this, but she still appears detached and sure of herself.

CATHY: Very well, think about it – and while you're thinking about it there's something I'd like you to remember.

LEONARD: (*Turning*) What's that, Miss White?

CATHY: It's not what you know about me that's important, Mr Harris – it's what I know about you.

LEONARD moves towards CATHY; he is massaging the palm of his right hand as he does so.

LEONARD: What is it you know about me?

CATHY: Well – for one thing, I know why you killed Charles Bannister.

LEONARD: (*Quietly*) Do you, my dear?

CATHY: He was getting too big for his shoes and he's started something else, something on his own. I don't know what it was. I don't know what he was playing at, but my guess is, whatever it was, you didn't like it!

LEONARD: (*Angrily*) You're damn right, I didn't like it! He was a pusher. He was peddling narcotics; he didn't want me to know about it, so he used a different name and pretended to be an invalid. (*Moving around*) The bloody fool! For a time, he had me worried – really worried! I was afraid the police would pick him up and he'd start talking. And believe me, he'd plenty to talk about …

CATHY: I can imagine.

LEONARD: (*Looking at CATHY*) Can you, my dear? (*He moves nearer to CATHY*) How much did Rupert tell you?

CATHY: About what?

LEONARD: About me – and my set-up?

177

CATHY: He told me how many girls were involved. One night, when he'd had too much to drink, he showed me the list, and the photographs.

LEONARD: Did he? What else did he show you?

CATHY: He told me about the property. He said you owned five houses down at …

LEONARD: Five? (*Laughing*) Five houses! Good God, he didn't know the half of it! If I had to tell you what property I own – how many girls I run – what my turnover was this month alone, you just wouldn't believe it!

The telephone suddenly rings. CATHY and LEONARD are both taken by surprise.

LEONARD: (*Tensely*) Let it ring …

CATHY: It's probably for Doreen …

LEONARD: It doesn't matter – let it ring …

The phone continues ringing and then stops. CATHY looks at LEONARD. She is now less sure of herself.

LEONARD: (*Quietly, massaging his hand*) Doreen Osborne told me you were a friend of my aunt's. A close friend.

CATHY: Yes, I know.

LEONARD: Is that true?

CATHY: No; I never even met Mrs Lincoln. I said that to Doreen because – well; I thought it would make you curious.

LEONARD: It did. I'm still curious. I want to know why you want to work for me? Why you need a job.

CATHY: Isn't it obvious why? I've very little money and I need a place to live. Besides, I know from what Rupert told me that you're …

LEONARD: I don't believe you … You're an operator … That's why you were able to handle Rupert … That's why you moved in with him.

CATHY: No! No, that's not true …
LEONARD: I think it is … Do you think I haven't met this
            situation before, for God's sake? Do you think
            it's new to me? (*Shaking his head and
            massaging his hand*) A girl overhears something
            – or finds out something – something about me.
            She feels important, it gives her a misguided
            sense of power and she suddenly takes the risk.
CATHY: What risk? What are you talking about?
LEONARD: I know what I'm talking about. Blackmail …
CATHY: I'm not trying to blackmail you, I wouldn't
            dream of …
LEONARD: Aren't you, Cathy? (*Softly*) I think you are … I
            think you are, you – (*Suddenly, tensely,
            tightening his right hand*) … dangerous little
            bitch!

*LEONARD suddenly moves towards CATHY, his hand raised.
CATHY, frightened and undecided what to do, instinctively
backs away from him. Suddenly, she turns and makes a dash
for the hall, but LEONARD quickly forestalls her by jumping
over the corner of the settee. He is now standing between
CATHY and the hall. CATHY backs away again – putting the
table and settee between herself and LEONARD.*

*LEONARD watches CATHY, trying to anticipate her next
move, his hand still raised – ready to strike. CATHY glances
across at the cocktail bar, as if about to turn in that direction.
She makes a sudden movement and as she does so LEONARD
springs forward and catches hold of her arm. For a brief
moment it looks as if LEONARD is going to hold on to her, then
CATHY struggles free and breathlessly takes up a position on
the opposite side of the table.*

*Angry – and intensely annoyed with himself – LEONARD
moves towards CATHY again. Suddenly, viciously his foot
shoots out, and the table topples over. As the table falls, they*

both move into new positions still facing each other – but with LEONARD now standing with his back to the cocktail bar.

LEONARD: You bitch …

LEONARD springs forward and catches hold of her; CATHY struggles, then realising that he is about to hit her, she throws herself at LEONARD – forcing him backwards onto the bar. This is a desperate move on CATHY's part and as LEONARD's body hits the counter JACK suddenly appears from behind the cocktail bar – his arm quickly encircling LEONARD's neck, pulling the astonished man violently backwards.

CATHY rushes to the bedroom and unlocks the door. ED ROYCE races out of the bedroom and joins JACK – hitting out wildly at the struggling LEONARD LINCOLN.

CUT TO: Outside Defoe Mansions. Day.

Several police cars are parked outside the entrance to the block of flats. JACK's car can be seen about twenty yards away. Uniformed men are standing by the cars watching the building. One of the drivers – TOM SMALL – is speaking on the car phone, his arm resting on the open window.

SMALL: (*On the phone*) … There's nothing to worry about, sir – it's all wrapped up. They're bringing him down now …

As SMALL speaks a uniformed policeman and a plain clothes detective emerge from the building with LEONARD LINCOLN. The uniformed men rush forward, and LINCOLN is quickly pushed into the car. As the police car races away, ED ROYCE appears with CATHY. As they reach the kerb, JACK comes out of the block of flats.

JACK: I'm sorry about that, I was talking to Bromford.

ED: I trust the Superintendent's pleased with our efforts?

JACK: Very. He seems highly delighted – they'll probably promote you, Ed.

180

ED: Or put me in charge of the canteen.

JACK laughs and taking CATHY by the arm puts her into his own car.

JACK: We'll see you later, old boy.

ED: (*Surprised, then with a suggestion of a smile*) Yes, all right, Jack.

JACK and CATHY drive off in the Austin 1100. Ed moves towards the police car and gets in.

CUT TO: Inside JACK's car.

JACK and CATHY are in the car. JACK is driving along at a steady speed.

JACK: ... Mrs Lincoln had several collars, they were specially made so she could conceal things in them. As a matter of fact, when Bannister kidnapped Midge, he found the photostat and the letter all the fuss was about. But he didn't tell Harris this – he thought it would be a good idea to have a hold over him. When Harris asked for the collar, Bannister gave him another one.

CATHY: The one Rupert had – the one I sent you?

JACK: Yes. (*Suddenly*) Cathy, what are you going to do now this business is over?

CATHY: I don't know. I've been offered a job in Manchester, but I don't know whether to take it or not. I thought I might go away for a week or two ...

JACK: That's a good idea. Why don't you go down to that place I told you about – Steeple Aston? It's quiet, it's a very nice hotel, and they're very nice people.

CATHY: Yes, I might do that. (*A moment*) I suppose you catch the train from Paddington?

JACK: (*Shaking his head*) No.

CATHY: (*Surprised*) No? Euston then?

181

JACK: You don't catch the train from anywhere. You talk a tall, handsome, intelligent Detective Inspector into driving you down there.

CATHY: Oh … But I'm not sure that I know one.

JACK looks at CATHY then starts laughing.

CUT TO: A Street in London. Day.

The Austin 1100 goes past.

THE END

Press Pack

press cuttings about A Game of Murder ...

The Lure on BBC2 – It's a new Durbridge (contains spoilers)

With effect from next Saturday viewers unable to receive BBC2 will be subjected to additional temptation to equip themselves to tune-in to the new channel.

The lure: a new Francis Durbridge serial.

It's called *A Game of Murder*, and it tells the story of Bob Kerry, a once famous professional athlete who now runs a sports shop in London.

When he is found dead on a golf course, his son Jack refuses to believe the coroner's verdict of misadventure.

In following up his suspicion he discovers secrets of his father's private life and finds that his search for the truth leads him to the world of call girls and the ruthless men who control them.

Gerald Harper stars as Jack, with June Barry and Conrad Phillips.

Liverpool Echo

Look Ahead

A Game of Murder, the latest thriller to be written by Erdington writer playwright Francis Durbridge, starts its BBC2 run on Saturday night. It is about call girls in London and the tough men who control them.

Leading parts will be played by Gerald Harper, June Barry and Conrad Phillips.

Durbridge mysteries are international best sellers. Because of overseas demands new techniques are to be introduced into the production of *A Game of Murder*. These will facilitate dubbing when recordings are sent abroad.

Birmingham Evening Mail

Durbridge Does It Again by **Marjorie Norris** (contains spoilers)

How deceptively easy Francis Durbridge makes it all seem! With the art that conceals art be began his latest thriller serial *A Game Of Murder* (BBC2 February 26th) with apparently irrelevant chatter at the start of a working day which might have been yours or mine. Fortunately for us it wasn't really our day, for within 25 minutes our alter ego Jack Kerry (Gerald Harper) was involved in two murders, mixed up in a mystery so mysterious that we can't hazard a guess at its nature, and well on the road to being under suspicion of bribery and corruption.

Scattered though the plot is, already, with red herrings and suspects, Francis Durbridge has embedded the story so deeply in prosaic routine and normal behaviour that nothing which has happened so far has put a strain on credibility. What could be more natural than that Mrs Lincoln (Dorothy Frere) should be worried about her missing poodle? What could be more natural than that Det. Insp. Jack Kerry should spare time from his own troubles to go and collect the dog from the pleasant couple (Diana King and John Harvey) who claimed to have it in their garden? What could be more natural than that Jack should agree to make out a cheque to some local charity rather than embarrass such a charming well-heeled couple with the advertised reward in cash?

Only we, the audience, on the alert for every hint of dirty work at the crossroads suspect everybody, see hidden motives in every word, every gesture, every smile. Francis Durbridge plays on us so skilfully that he has us doing some of the work for him.

The cast showed their awareness of this – each overplaying by that minute fraction that confirmed us in our suspicions that all was not as it seemed and that the comforting ordinariness of the opening was but a thin crust that would crack and plunge

Jack Kerry into the unknown. Gerald Harper's policeman-victim is cast in the anti-hero role mould: edgy, impatient, overworked. The friction between him and Chief. Insp. Bromford (Conrad Phillips) sparked like an electric arc.

Two people most regrettably already written out are Anthony Sagar (killed off very early on but not before he had endeared himself to me as Jack Kerry's father) and Murray Hayne (so convincingly distraught at having caused that death by accident that it was instantly clear to the students of thrillers that he was next to go on the list of dear departed). Making up the rest of the cast of the first episode were Christopher Wray, Lesley Carole, Donald Oliver, David Burke, June Barry and Bernard G. High. Frankly, I don't trust any of them – not even the police.

Television Today